# PRETENSES

# TRESSIE LOCKWOOD

AMIRA PRESS

**False**
PRETENSES

Amira Press
Charlotte, NC
www.amirapress.com

# Chapter One

lyssa paced outside the double glass doors, wringing her hands. Butterflies knotted her stomach, and she swallowed over and over to try to wet her dry throat. Every time someone passed the entrance on the other side of the doors, she ducked to the side against the wall to remain unseen. When she had first stepped off the elevator, she'd spotted the receptionist strolling away from her desk, but the woman hadn't returned yet. With a thriving corporation like the one her cousin worked for, no doubt someone had to monitor the entrance for guests at all times. She couldn't stay out here forever.

*Okay, Alyssa, this isn't a big deal. Pull yourself together. Trinity is not going to turn you down. She can't.* As much as she gave herself the pep talk, nothing helped to alleviate her trepidation. No, more than fear kept her in the hall outside her cousin's workplace. She hated having to ask Trinity for help, or anyone else for that matter. She had considered herself to be the more successful of the two of them having started her own business five years ago. Trinity went the route of working for someone else, and now she had a nice salary and benefits, while Alyssa faced losing her bookstore, which she'd worked her fingers to the bone to maintain.

Somewhere nearby an elevator dinged, but not on that floor. Soon enough someone would come along, and she would need to explain why she stood in the hall like a stalker or a thief. She sucked in a deep breath and straightened her back. A hand dropped on her shoulder, and she squeaked.

"I'm sorry to startle you, Alyssa," came the deep, rumbling voice. "Are you okay?"

She turned in degrees, her stomach flip-flopping. Of all people to catch her, it had to be Trinity's boss—the very sexy, very single billionaire—Nathan Corde.

"Nathan, how are you?" She forced a smile. "Yes, I'm fine, thanks. I was just…" Absolutely nothing came to mind to cover for her weird behavior. He waited with raised eyebrows and a polite expression of interest, which she assumed would fizzle soon. The fact that he remembered her name meant nothing, especially since he was the kind of corporate man who used a trick to recall everyone's name even after the briefest of meetings, or so Trinity had told her. Alyssa and he had run into each other less than a handful of times since her cousin started with his company. Alyssa had always done no more than say hello and enjoy the view.

Nathan smiled, and she lost focus for a second in his dimples and the crinkling of his hazel eyes. Added to this devastation, when he tilted his head downward to focus on her, his dark brown hair tumbled onto his forehead in a movement that gave him at first a rakish look and then a boyish one. How that was possible, she didn't know. All she put together in her befuddled mind was the man could stop a woman's heart with that smile, and as nice as he always seemed, she bet he knew it.

*Okay, seriously, where's the bitterness coming from?*

"I'm just here to see my cousin really quick," she mumbled.

"Of course, you're always welcome." He laid a hand at her lower back and gestured toward the entrance to the executive suite. "You don't have to wait out here. Come inside. Trinity should have gotten back here before I did after we finished with our meeting."

Alyssa tried ignoring the sensations generated from his hand on her body, even if her blouse did separate their skin from touching. "Oh, no worries. I just got here and was checking my messages before going in." Why couldn't that excuse have come to mind sooner, before she looked like a fool in front of him?

To her slight disappointment, Nathan didn't stay long at her side. He escorted her past the reception area to the back, where Trinity's office sat outside his. He flashed her another smile, said some words she didn't pay attention to, then disappeared behind his office door. Alyssa sighed at the loss of the eye candy and sank into the chair in front of Trinity's desk. While her cousin gave a quick wave and continued her conversation on the phone, Alyssa glanced around like she always did.

3

The office was well-appointed in shades of wine, cream, and brown. The walls held beautiful landscapes, and the carpet was so thick, no sound emanated when crossing it. Trinity's desk stretched wide, but it didn't eclipse the space of her office at all. Everything screamed money, but nice as it was, it didn't touch Nathan's space beyond. Trinity had taken Alyssa inside to show off the wall of windows overlooking the street below. The city view both amazed and unsettled her.

When Trinity raised her voice, shouting into the phone, Alyssa sat up and paid attention. Before she could catch more than a couple of words, her cousin hung up. Anger contorted her expression, and she thrust her chair back from the desk.

"Trin, you okay?"

Her cousin glared at her and began to pace. "Of course not. I mean…" She drew in a breath and blew it out. "I'm fine. What's up? I thought we were doing lunch next week."

Alyssa's stomach knotted again. "Yeah, I know, but something came up. Well, it didn't *just* come up, but I couldn't wait until next week, especially since you're always rescheduling. I wanted to talk to you as soon as possible. Trinity, I need a favor."

Her cousin's lips curled on one side. "What kind of favor?"

"I need money to save my business. I'll pay you back. I promise. I have some ideas to modernize the store, and I know it will turn things around."

"Tell me you're not talking about that bookstore."

Alyssa ground her teeth. "You know that's the only business I have, Trin. It's my life. I kept it going for five

4

years, and they say if a business can make it that long, it stands a great chance for success."

"No."

"Wait, let me explain some of my plans. This is a loan, not a gift. I even drew up a schedule for making payments, which would start in about six months, if that's okay."

Trinity ran a hand over her face and walked to where Alyssa sat. She touched her cheek in a gesture of affection. Irritation rose in Alyssa, and she fought the urge to smack her cousin's hand away. All she needed was a yes.

"I'm sorry, girl," Trinity said. "I love you like a sister. We grew up together, and I'll always be there for you, but not for this. As far as I'm concerned, that bookstore is an ending waiting to happen. It's held you back for five years. You're smart. You can do so much more."

"*This* is what I want to do—run the bookstore. I'm living my dream!"

A harsh laugh escaped Trinity. "You call what you do living? Your apartment is in the worst part of the city. You could have stayed with Dad and done something better with the money you inherited from your parents when they died. Instead, you threw it all away on this money pit, and now you want me to throw good money after bad."

"You're a cold-blooded, bitch, you know that?" The moment the words left her mouth, Alyssa slapped a hand over her lips. No way Trinity would help her after such an insult. She searched for words to rectify the situation along with convincing her cousin to change her mind. "Trin, *please*."

Before Trinity could comment, the phone rang at her

5

desk. She glared at Alyssa and then leaned across the desk to answer it. Alyssa didn't move from the spot where she sat. She couldn't afford to leave the office without help. The bank had already turned her down for a loan. Trinity had the money. She knew that, and she was Alyssa's last hope. If she could just find the right words to convince her, she would not lose the one thing that belonged to her in the world. Trinity couldn't understand what this meant to her.

Her cousin's distraught voice pulled her from her thoughts for the second time. "Look, I told you it's just part of the job. Please, Curtis. I thought you would understand."

The tremor in her cousin's voice struck pain in Alyssa's chest. Curtis, Trinity's boyfriend, hung the moon, if Trinity told the story. She loved the man to distraction and did anything he asked. He treated Trinity like gold, but he had one flaw that Alyssa saw. His jealousy knew no bounds.

Sitting so close to Trinity's desk, Alyssa couldn't help but pick up her side of the conversation.

"I'm just pretending to be his girlfriend for a week," her cousin explained.

Alyssa's eyes widened until they hurt. What the heck could they be discussing? Who was she pretending to date, and why?

Trinity went on. "I don't understand why you're tripping, Curtis. It's not like we'll be sleeping together, and I've gone with him on business trips before. You didn't have a problem then. His parents are going to be there. He wants to get them off his back. No, he's not gay!"

Alyssa pressed a hand to her mouth to keep from laughing. She figured out Trinity and her boyfriend discussed

Nathan. Why in the world would he need a woman to pretend to be his girlfriend? If, as Trinity said, Nathan's parents would be wherever they intended to fly, then wouldn't it be more volatile to bring home a black woman than to just show up alone? Maybe he was gay and still in the closet. The thought of that disappointed her somehow. Not that she'd ever get a chance with him or would even try to.

When Trinity began to cry, an idea struck Alyssa. Guilt knotted her stomach, but she ignored it. As far as she could see, this was a win-win-win situation, and one Trinity couldn't refuse.

At last, Trinity hung up the phone, and Alyssa guessed it wouldn't be the last time Curtis called to harass her about her decision to play her boss's girlfriend. Trinity walked around her desk and sat down to check her makeup. "I'm sorry, Alyssa. I'm not in the mood to fight with you too. I'll call you tonight if you want, and we can talk more."

Alyssa slid forward in her chair and pinned her cousin with a narrowed stare. "I'll do it."

Trinity blinked at her. "Do what?"

"I'll pretend to be Nathan's girlfriend. If this isn't business—because I type with two fingers and don't take dictation—I will play his girlfriend. We look a lot alike, so if it's about his parents already seeing a picture of you, then..."

"They've never seen me." A dazed expression crossed Trinity's face.

"Then it's perfect. You said a week, right?"

Trinity frowned. "Why would you do this? You don't even like Curtis."

Alyssa rolled her eyes. "I don't hate him. Y'all are just so lovey-dovey most of the time, it makes a person sick. He's a decent guy, and even though he wants your attention twenty-four seven, he treats you right. I don't have a problem with him."

"Okay, I get that much, but this is a big favor. Nathan didn't even want to ask me. Just like you, I overheard him talking to his mother about the trip. He might be ruthless when it comes to business, but he respects them, and they drive him nuts about settling down. He didn't say so, but I'm thinking he wants to shock them with bringing a black woman as a potential wife."

"Shock them?"

"Yeah, into realizing he can't just grab any woman off the street. She has to be the right one."

Alyssa cringed. "So you were going as the money-grubbing gold digger?"

"No, he's not like that." Trinity considered it. "Well, maybe *they* are. Money does run in the family. I didn't even think of it that way until you mentioned it. I'm used to being respected around here because I work for Nathan. Wow, maybe he should find another way."

"No!" Alyssa cleared her throat and calmed down. "I mean, he's a good man and great boss, as you keep saying. He wouldn't allow his family to mistreat his girlfriend even if she is a fake. Let me do this. I can spare a week, and you can keep your relationship."

Trinity folded her arms under her breasts. "In exchange for what?"

Alyssa smiled. "You already know. In exchange for the loan."

"Are you serious? It's not that big of an issue. Besides, if your business is failing, how can you afford to close it down for a week?"

"My business is not failing." She ground her teeth. "I hired a part-time manager recently. She can do full time for the week I'm not there."

Trinity's doubt in her sanity radiated. "You hired a manager?"

"She has over twenty years of experience and great ideas for growth."

Her cousin shook her head in disbelief. "You know this is crazy, right?"

Alyssa stood up, certain she had gotten what she wanted. "I have to get back to the store. Call me tonight with the details. Oh, and make it crystal clear to your boss that I am not selling my body in exchange for the loan. In fact, let's keep that part between us. This is just pretend. Okay?"

Trinity sighed and stood as well. "Against my better judgment, you've got a deal. Have fun in the Cayman Islands."

# Chapter Two

Alyssa fidgeted with her seat belt, her hands shaking so much and her head spinning until she thought she would pass out. Beside her, Nathan laid a hand over hers, and she was struck, not for the first time since they started out on this trip, by the difference in their skin tones. Nathan's tanned flesh contrasted with her coffee-with-cream brown. She had never considered dating a white man. As far as he and others of his race were concerned, she enjoyed looking, but never sampling.

"Are you feeling okay?" he asked, cutting into her thoughts.

She jerked at his touch but resisted pulling away, and concern colored his expression. They hadn't gotten off the ground in New York yet, and here she was blowing it. "I'm sorry."

"You'll have to do better than that," he chided.

"I—"

He squeezed her hand and brought it to his lips. She stared at him, watching as he brushed her palm. A zing of desire rocketed through her body and straight down between her legs.

"You'll have to learn to be more comfortable around me," he explained. "We'll have to look like we're in love. If I can't touch your hand or even kiss you without you running away from me, we'll be found out."

"K-Kiss me?" Of course he intended to kiss her. They had discussed it over dinner when he insisted he take her out to go over the details of what he expected and what she would not put up with. She must have been insane to do this, but Trinity had agreed to give her a check as soon as she arrived back in New York. The deal had been struck, and there wasn't anything she wouldn't do for her dream. "Of course, kiss. What was I thinking? You're right. I'll do better."

She peered up through her lashes at him and didn't miss the doubt marking his handsome face. Determined to prove he didn't have the wrong woman for the job, she leaned over and touched her lips to his in a brief peck. The fleeting contact raised goose bumps along her arms and sent new pings of need to her nether regions, but Nathan appeared less than impressed.

He frowned. "That's the kind of kiss you give to a friend."

"You kiss your friends on the lips?"

He tipped her chin up. "You need to do it like you mean it. I don't believe you love me, Alyssa."

*Damn, this man plays hardball. What was I thinking?*

She licked her lips and swallowed, trying to get sharp control of her senses, but Nathan didn't make it easy. Staring into those eyes threatened to rob her of equilibrium, and staying silent didn't put him off. He waited for her response.

After an eternity, he released her and turned away. Alyssa blew out a sigh of relief.

"This is why we are arriving a day early," he informed her. "To get you ready."

"So you're not having any trouble at all? You're okay with kissing some random woman?"

He chuckled. "You're not some random woman. You're Trinity's cousin, and even if you weren't, you're very beautiful. Why wouldn't I enjoy kissing you?"

Her throat went dry at the offhand compliment. "Thank you. I think."

"Mr. Corde, would you like a drink, sir?" The flight attendant, with clear interest in Nathan, leaned over his seat. Alyssa wondered if the woman always worked for Nathan or if she'd been borrowed from another airline. At least when this trip ended, Alyssa would have an incredible memory. Never in her wildest dreams did she ever think she'd fly on a private jet.

"I'll have a Suburban," Nathan said. "And you, honey?"

Alyssa just caught herself from starting at the endearment. The woman waited with a polite expression that didn't light her eyes. Alyssa rested a hand on Nathan's arm in a possessive move designed to piss her off. She almost laughed at the attendant's cringe. "I'll have a Cosmopolitan, if you don't mind. Thanks."

"Sure," came the tight reply, and she turned away.

"Good girl," Nathan whispered in her ear, sending chills racing each other down her spine. When her drink came, she took a few fortifying sips and relaxed in her seat while they hurtled toward an experience she wasn't sure she was ready for.

⁓

A man in a dark chauffeur's uniform waited for them in the baggage claiming area. Alyssa was surprised the vehicle they rode in wasn't a limo, but the town car was nice all the same. When they pulled up before a hotel that could be nothing other than five star, she turned to him. "I thought we were staying at your family home."

He slid from the car and held out a hand to her when the driver opened the door for him. Alyssa put her hand in his, not startled this time at the tingle.

"We will tomorrow," he explained. "While we're getting to know each other better, I don't want to be under the watchful eyes of the staff."

She blinked. "Staff?"

"Yes, it's a large home. Since my father and I are usually busy with work-related issues even while on vacation, and my mother and sister have their pursuits, someone needs to cook and clean. We hire staff to do that. We've had the same people come in seasonally to work for us. They're locals."

Alyssa thought of the apartment she rented, which Trinity had insulted. She'd spoken the truth when she said Alyssa lived in a higher crime area, but it was all she could afford. New York was an expensive city no matter where one chose to reside. She wanted to do better, and hopefully with the loan and changes made to her store, she could in time.

Nathan wrapped Alyssa's fingers around his arm and guided her into the hotel. After checking in, she was glad to find the suite he'd booked held separate bedrooms. She counted three along with a kitchen, living room, and dining room.

"Are we expecting anyone else?" she asked, bewildered.

"No."

"It's a bit much for one night." She strolled to the middle of the suite that was larger and nicer than her apartment and stood there. Behind her, Nathan thanked and tipped the bellman. The door *whooshed* shut, and the automatic lock clicked into place.

"Come here, Alyssa."

She peered at him over her shoulder. He held out a hand, causing her heart to hammer.

"Please."

All of sudden, she forgot how to walk as she stumbled to him. He stood in the hall, off the kitchen, and she joined him there. When his hands settled on her arms, she shivered. He stroked her skin with a featherlight touch.

"The more I touch you, the more comfortable you'll be."

She swallowed. "You're not going to try to seduce me, are you? Because you're not my type."

His brows went up at her bald statement. Maybe he believed every woman wanted him. The way she shook and panted being this close to him, he would know the truth just looking at her. She did her best to pull it together.

"I don't plan on it. But you're telling me you feel nothing when I do this?" He raised her chin, leaned down, and kissed her lips, a touch that was a far cry from what she'd attempted on the plane.

When he raised his head, she thanked the heavens for her cocoa skin so he couldn't see her flush. "It's not bad or anything."

He winced.

*Score one for me.*

"Well, I guess I will have to try harder." He came in for another kiss, but she wriggled out of his grasp and hurried away.

"Which of these rooms is mine? I need to get cleaned up, and I would love to take a quick nap before dinnertime."

She expected him to protest, but he let her go and pointed her in the right direction. Alyssa found her bags already settled at the base of the bed and shut her door to go through one of them. For a good ten minutes, she sorted through her clothing while her mind raced with thoughts of Nathan Corde's lips. They'd been warm and soft, and he tasted better than any lover she'd ever had. *Wait, don't even go there, girl. He is not now, and never will be, your lover. Period.*

How would things have gone if it were Trinity? She loved Curtis, but could she pretend to love Nathan, and would she have flinched at his kisses? Alyssa sat on the bed. Maybe this entire fiasco was just that, a ruse for Nathan to get a black woman in his bed. Then again, that was absurd. The man stood several inches over six feet and had a body most men would pay good money to have, not to mention he was rich. Women of all kinds would line up to share his bed.

Still mulling it over, she climbed into the shower and washed off. After she'd lotioned her skin and folded into a thick robe provided by the hotel, she lay across the bed. Because she hadn't been able to sleep the night before, tiredness weighed heavy on her, and soon she drifted off into dreamland.

A hand stroking her hair woke her, and she swatted at it without opening her eyes. "Never touch a black woman's hair without permission," she muttered.

"Is that true?" came the curious reply.

Memory of where she was and who sat on the side of her bed came flooding back, and she popped up. "Nathan!"

"I'm sorry. You didn't answer my knock, so I came in. It's after six, and I wanted to check to see if you were hungry. We can go out, or I can arrange for a chef to come in and cook for us. Your choice." While he spoke, his gaze dropped from her face to her chest. Too late, she remembered she'd thrown the robe on after her shower and nothing else. The garment gaped open, exposing the beginning swell of her breasts. One move would uncover a nipple, and Nathan had noticed. Alyssa jerked the robe closed and jumped to her feet.

"Yes, thanks for waking me. I'm starving. We can go out unless you want to stay in? I want to see the island at night."

"Your wish is my command."

When they stepped out of the hotel, a limo waited, and Nathan dismissed the driver from holding the door for her and did it himself. She thanked him and moved past, making every effort not to brush him as she folded into the dark interior.

"Do you travel often by limo?"

He smiled. "Not always. I have a couple of cars I tool around in now and then. The limo is convenient for getting work done without the hindrance of watching the road."

She nodded. "I balance the books on the train into work. It's convenient."

When he gave a polite response, she wondered if he'd ever been on public transportation.

The restaurant Nathan chose was a beautiful whitewashed building, which, as nice as it appeared outside, took Alyssa's breath away inside. Purple, blue, and white lights illuminated walls covered in simplistic but skillful artwork. None of the paintings were in actual frames, but each looked to have been created directly on the wall, and they connected in a way that brought a sense of peace and warmth over her just gazing at them. A bar with neon blue lights beneath the counter stretched along one wall, and tables covered with pristine white tablecloths had been arranged around the floor.

A host in crisp uniform stepped up to greet them. "Mr. Corde, it's good to see you again, sir. I hope you're doing well this evening?"

"Jeff, good, thanks." Nathan shook the man's hand, and as they were led farther into the restaurant, she overheard someone else informing another host that they had reservations. When she and Nathan were seated in a private room, she studied him in curiosity.

"Did you make reservations?"

His brows went up. "I have a standing reservation here."

"Standing?" She unfolded the cloth napkin and laid it across her lap. So much silverware framed her plate, she wondered which was proper, and then didn't care. "Oh, you mean they will oust anyone because it's you?"

Rather than answer, Nathan turned to the waiter who approached their table. Again the two men seemed to know each other by name. Alyssa allowed Nathan to choose what she drank for the evening, and then she perused the menu. No prices were listed. *A sign it costs an arm and a leg, I bet.*

"So why are you doing this?" she questioned him when they were alone.

"You get right to the point, don't you?"

She shrugged. "I don't bite my tongue. Well, usually. I like to know where I stand, and I can't help wondering if you just want a black woman in your bed. Maybe you have a thing for Trinity, but she ruined your plans by backing out at the last minute. You couldn't very well admit the whole pretend boyfriend-girlfriend thing was a lie."

He reached across the table and took her hand. Her fingers spasmed in his hold, and she jerked away. Nathan turned his hand over, palm up, and waited. With great effort, she placed hers back in his, and his thumb stroked her skin in gentle, slow circles.

"No, I am not interested in Trinity. I know she has a boyfriend. I do not horn in on another man's territory. There are too many single women in the world."

She clenched her teeth and lowered her gaze to the table.

19

"I have had sex with a black woman before. It was brief and enjoyable, a one-night stand. We remain acquaintances, and I imagine if I gave any indication I wanted to continue, she would be willing."

*No confidence in himself at all.* She just kept herself from rolling her eyes.

"While I'm free to come and go whenever and wherever I choose, I would not create a trip such as this just to get into a woman's panties."

"Okay, so my logic's off," she said. "And you can get whatever woman you want."

He narrowed his eyes and at last released her. Alyssa buried her hands in her lap while struggling to calm the sensations he had evoked.

"You seem angry at me. I understood that you volunteered to take Trinity's place."

She gasped. "You don't think…I mean, I never meant to imply…"

"No, Trinity made that clear. Don't worry. I know you're not available for anything other than pretense, but I'm curious. Do you have a boyfriend?"

She bit her lip. "No. He…*I*…broke it off a few weeks ago. We weren't right for each other." She didn't care to tell him Tony had suggested an open relationship and informed her he never wanted kids. Two blows in one. He hadn't cheated, he said, but the fact that he wanted to see other people while still having her said he eventually would. "So what about you? Surely, there was, or is, someone special in your life that you can take to meet your parents, and if not, why pretend? Isn't that giving them false hope?"

"There isn't." He seemed to hesitate, but she wouldn't let him get out of giving her a straight answer. When he tapped the table in a decisive movement, she realized he wasn't the type to back off of a challenge. "My father has terminal cancer."

Alyssa gaped. That was the last thing she had expected to hear. "I'm so sorry."

He nodded his thanks. "They both want grandchildren more than anything at this point, and my sister, for her own reasons, refuses to give in to the demand, so to speak. That leaves me."

"And you don't want kids either?" The truth hurt even though she had no designs on him. Just knowing another man who stepped all over her own dream got to her.

"It's not that I don't want them. I need a wife, but I'm not ready to find one." He shrugged. "However, my father means a lot to me, and I want to make his last days happy. If he thinks I'm close to getting married and having kids, that will be enough for him."

Tears welled in Alyssa's eyes. "I understand that."

"I chose you, or rather Trinity, when it occurred to me that a white woman wouldn't do."

Alyssa stared. The logic escaped her in this instance.

"I can see you think I'm crazy. Think about it. I'm thirty-five. Over the years, my father has seen me date or have a fling with one blonde after another, a few brunettes thrown in here and there, but all of a certain type."

*So in other words, you're a man whore who likes the leggy, empty-headed model type.* She tried not to show her conclusion in her expression, but something told her she failed when he chuckled. Nathan didn't care one bit what she thought of him, and he had made no bones about admitting his love of women.

"He won't believe it's real if you bring home the same kind of woman," she said.

"No, he won't, and I thought, what type of woman could be extreme enough for him to think at last I had succumbed to love?"

"Trinity."

"You," he corrected.

Trinity had gone to college and held a master's in communication. She hobnobbed with rich people every day and held her own. She'd never take down to any of them. Alyssa realized she would make the perfect candidate for Nathan to take home. Alyssa's bachelor's in English literature did nothing to enhance her career since one didn't need to have a command of Shakespeare to sell erotic romance books or "how to build your own furniture" manuals. The average Joe frequented her store, and she had only ever rubbed elbows with the working middle class.

"I don't want to bring up race, but if you're thirty-five, your parents have to be in their fifties?"

"Sixties."

He didn't appear offended, so she continued. "Won't they have a problem with you getting serious with a black woman? Even younger people sometimes have issues, despite seeing more and more mixed couples these days. I wouldn't want to upset your dad. I respect people's opinions. I just don't have to deal with them."

"I've thought about it, but I believe with the crisis we're dealing with, he won't care. After Trinity agreed to come with me, I mentioned to my mother over the phone that she's African American. My mother sounded surprised and a little taken aback. I know she told my father, but I heard no more about it. Mom called me several times after that to make sure I was still coming and bringing you."

"Are you insane?" she squeaked. "So you don't know what we're walking into. They could be planning a family intervention."

He burst out laughing. "Don't worry."

"I am worried, damn it."

He reached across the table and touched her cheek just as their food arrived. Alyssa found her fears escalating, both because she couldn't shake the attraction to this man and for whatever waited at his family's vacation home. All she knew was even if his parents came at her wrong, she couldn't cuss them out with his father so ill. No way would she cause the early death of an old man. With each passing moment, she wondered if this was the stupidest mistake she'd ever made.

# Chapter Three

"eady?"

Nathan held out his hand, and Alyssa slipped her sandals off and then took it. From the first step, her feet sank into the warm white sand, and she followed him along the beach. As they strolled, the sun glowed orange on the horizon, creating a breathtaking view. The night breeze brought the scent of mangoes and lime, and she inhaled it, allowing the atmosphere to ease away some of her worry and stress.

"What about you?" he asked after a few moments of silence.

"Me?"

He nodded. "Over dinner I told you a little of my family. I'd like to learn more about you, and if possible, help you to relax."

She ducked her head, annoyed he could pick up on how tense she'd been. All through dinner, as they discussed various light subjects, she hadn't been able to get his family off her mind, especially his father. On top of that, knowing she had to perform for all of them tangled her stomach even more. Sure, she'd been desperate enough to volunteer for this madness, but in the face of it, the situation had changed.

Nathan squeezed her hand to bring her back to the present, and she sighed. "Nothing much to tell. I have no siblings, and I grew up with Trinity and her dad and stepmom."

His eyebrows rose in the waning light. "Your parents?"

"They were killed in a plane crash when I was ten."

"I'm sorry."

She thanked him, and while the tragedy had happened eighteen years ago, she still felt a strong sense of loss at not having a mother.

"What was that like?"

His question surprised her. Most people on hearing she'd been orphaned at a young age shied away from the subject. Studying Nathan, she tried determining if he was insensitive or just nosey. His calm expression gave few real clues, and since she had no reason to ignore him, she answered his query.

"It wasn't bad. I mean, after my initial grief and depression. Trinity's dad is an awesome man. He loved me like a daughter, and he offered to let me live in his house forever, even after I grew up. He's not a blood relationship to me. Trinity's mother was my mother's sister, but she left them early on, and he remarried when Trinity was five. Even after my mother died, she never came to the funeral or to see us."

"I didn't know she had such a past. When she mentions her mother, she sounds like she loves her very much."

"Her stepmom," Alyssa agreed, "she's pretty special, but I was determined to stand on my own two feet, and when I found out I had a small inheritance from my parents, I used it to start my business."

"Interesting. I would enjoy hearing more about your business." He stopped walking and faced her. "For now, since we don't have a lot of time, I think we should practice a little more."

All the relaxation Alyssa had achieved went floating away over the waves of the ocean. When he laid gentle hands on her upper arms, a tremor passed through her that was not all nervousness. He drew her close, and she peered up at him through her lashes. She could say no and tell him they didn't need all these displays of affection to appear to be in love. Everyone wasn't that open. The problem was, she wanted to kiss him again, and deeper than the last time.

She licked her lips and waited, but he didn't close the space between them. Was he nervous as well? Getting bold, she let her sandals fall to the sand and rose up on the balls of her feet. Her hands on his chest, she leaned in and touched her lips to his. Nathan's hand roamed from her arms to her waist, and he tugged her to him. His lips parted above hers, and the moment his tongue touched the tip of hers, he swept her away on a cloud of yearning that made her cream her panties. *Back up, Alyssa. You don't know what you're doing, girl.*

She pressed tighter to his chest and slid her palms along the contours of his hard muscle. Taut nipples met her fingertips, and she came close to losing her breath. Nathan nudged her chin even higher and deepened the kiss. His tongue snaked along the insides of her mouth and curled with her tongue. A moan rose in her throat, but she tamped it down. At last, she found the strength to pull back, but he sucked a bit, a move that caught her bottom lip between his. The sounds they made when they separated had her wanting to go back, but she stepped out of his hold.

"That was more like it," he commented, amusement in his tone.

She glared at him. "It was more than necessary. I doubt you'll need to put your tongue down my throat while your family's around."

"Would be convincing."

"Not on your life, pal."

He grinned and stuffed his hands in his pockets, but not before she spotted the tent there. She turned her back on him and rubbed a hand over her mouth. When she bent to get her sandals, he beat her to them, stooping way too close. He took his time straightening, and to keep from looking like the scaredy-cat she felt, she held her stance, refusing to be intimidated. Nathan's suppressed grin and raised eyebrows said he recognized the act for what it was.

"You said you just ended a relationship?" His gaze steadied on her face.

"You're insinuating I'm inexperienced?" She tilted her head to the side and placed a hand on her hip, challenging him. The sexy eyes crinkled at the ends.

"I would never." He reached out to grasp a lock of her hair and twirled it around his finger. "From that kiss, I think it's safe to say you're not new to the game."

"Oh, it's a game, huh?"

"It can be."

Alyssa began walking, and Nathan fell into step beside her. She kept her attention on putting one foot in front of the other because just as he had insinuated, that kiss had lit her on fire. All she could do was fight to keep her hands to herself and not suggest to him that they go back to his room. She wasn't into jumping into bed with men she had just met, and while Nathan wasn't exactly new, he was Trinity's boss. That could make things awkward for her cousin, and Trinity didn't deserve it.

"Why did you agree to come with me, if you don't mind my asking?"

She stumbled, and his hand shot out to catch her before she fell. Yes, she did mind him asking. Stalling, she pushed her hair back from her face when a breeze stirred it. "I told you I grew up with Trinity. Doing this favor for you meant a lot to her, and for her it meant a lot to me. She's been there for me when I needed her. I wanted to give back in a way that I could."

He listened in attentiveness to her explanation, and while he nodded when she finished, she wondered if he believed it. Then she decided she didn't care if he did or didn't. Her money issues were her problem, and a man like him couldn't understand anyway. After some moments, he reached out and threaded his fingers with hers. She tried pulling away, but he held on.

"There will be times we walk along the beach with my family present. A couple in love wants to touch each other often." He raised her hand to his mouth and kissed it. She shivered, and he frowned in concern. "Are you cold?"

"Um, no. I'm good, thanks."

He tugged her to his side and wrapped an arm about her shoulders. This time she didn't flinch or pull away. Deciding she wanted this to work, she nuzzled in under his arm and laid her head against his shoulder. They moved as one, taking slow steps. *I bet to anyone looking we seem like a couple.* She peered up at his face. *What would it be like to love a man like him?*

"Shouldn't I know more about you, like your routine?" she asked.

He snapped his fingers. "You're right. Come. We'll sit down here and study."

They found beach chairs, and Nathan brushed the seats free of sand. For the next few hours, they sat together sharing some intimate and some boring details of their everyday lives.

"I own a bookstore," Alyssa confessed, "and I never thought we'd have anything in common, but I guess we're both workaholics."

Nathan agreed. "We don't get a lot of time to spend together, so we cherish what we can."

She ducked her head. He spoke as if they really were a couple. The man had the acting thing down pat. "I text you just to say I love you at various times of the day."

He fingered her palm. That was the kind of thing she dreamed of having with someone, a closeness that reached across space and time, trust and loyalty that didn't waver. Would Nathan be faithful to the woman he dated, or would he tell her up front she would never be the only one?

"I'm not into open relationships," she blurted, and he started in surprise.

"Neither am I. I do not share my woman." Switching directions, he added, "My favorite food is French fries."

She laughed. "Seriously?"

"Does that seem weird?"

"I don't know. You don't look like the French fry type."

"Meaning?"

He didn't appear to be offended, so she told him the truth. "The corporate kind of man who knows which of the fancy forks to use when at a formal dinner."

His boyish smile took her breath away. "Ah, but that's the appeal of the French fry. You can't enjoy it unless you eat it with your fingers."

"And it's not good if it's not a little greasy."

"Agreed!"

After another hour or so of getting to know each other, Alyssa began nodding off, and Nathan rose and dragged her to her feet. By now his arms around her had started to feel normal and comfortable.

"Time for bed," he announced.

She yawned, leaning on his chest, and they strolled back to the room. "Good night," Alyssa murmured and stumbled into her room. She shut and locked the door and then leaned on it. Even the chilly panel didn't cool her hot body. Everything about him excited her, from his smile, to his voice, to his eyes, and his touch...

She didn't know how she would bear the coming week. At least if she revealed her attraction, she could put it down to great acting. If nothing else, she needed to guard her heart and know, in the end, it would all benefit her business.

❧

In the late afternoon, Alyssa and Nathan checked out of the hotel and were driven to another location. When Alyssa stepped into the lobby of the new place, she wrinkled her nose in confusion and turned to Nathan. "I thought we were going to your parents' house? What's the name of this hotel?"

He grinned, leaning down to whisper in her ear, "This is our family estate here in the islands."

Embarrassment and wonder washed over her at the same time. The ground floor where they stood spread out so open and big, it rivaled the best and most expensive of hotels. Just past the front door, an arrangement of real palm trees stretched up from the first floor almost to the third. Double dark oak doors lined the walls on the first and second floor, while windows lined those of the third. One side of the third led off into some other part of the house. The very fact that she saw all of this from where she stood blew her mind.

While she wanted to continue to gawk at the house that must be worth millions, a maid glided down the stairs and approached them. Her straight back and serviceable uniform impressed Alyssa all the more. "Mr. Corde, welcome home, sir."

"Talia, thank you," Nathan responded. "This is my girlfriend, Alyssa. Can you show her to her room?"

The woman didn't bat an eyelash at the fact that Alyssa's skin was as brown as hers. She smiled and nodded her greeting. Alyssa found her voice and answered in kind.

"Mrs. Corde gave instructions for Ms. Alyssa to be placed in your room, sir. Aziz has already taken the luggage up. Ms. Alyssa, I'll show you the way."

"Wait, in Nathan's room?" Alyssa squeaked.

Nathan cleared his throat. Before either of them could speak further, a woman called out from behind them, and Alyssa and Nathan turned. The woman hurrying up the few steps to the doorway appeared to be an older female version of Nathan. Alyssa knew this must be his mother.

"Nathan, darling," she cooed and raised her cheek for Nathan to kiss. He did so and drew his mother in for a warm hug. She didn't reach beyond his shoulder, but her fiery spirit made her seem taller. "Dad and I have missed you. I wish you would visit more often."

"I promise I will," he assured her and drew Alyssa to his side. "Mom, this is Alyssa. Alyssa, my mom."

"You can call me Lydia, dear," his mother said.

She offered a cheek to Alyssa too, and Alyssa gave her a brief hug and a sort of half-cheek, half-air kiss. The fact that real people greeted each other this way surprised her, but she did her best to recover quickly so she wouldn't embarrass Nathan or look like a poor gawking tourist.

"It's nice to meet you, Mrs....um...Lydia. Thank you for inviting me to your home."

Lydia waved a hand and turned back toward the door. "When Dad gets his second wind, he'll come in. Of course, he only likes Aziz to help him. Oh, here is Aziz. Aziz, help Mr. Corde in, will you?"

"Of course, ma'am." The young man, about thirty or

33

so, who had Talia's eyes and nose, swept out the door in brisk efficiency.

Lydia had them all seated in a living room off the main area and Talia away for refreshments in a heartbeat. Alyssa soon crossed her legs with a glass of iced tea, having declined the hot equivalent on a day like today. Nathan took her free hand and laced his fingers with hers.

"Mom, I think Talia made a mistake and put us in the same room," Nathan began.

"Oh pish." His mother rolled her eyes. "I may not be young, but I'm not stupid, Nathan. I know what you young people get up to these days before marriage. I will have you know I'm not completely old-fashioned. I told Talia to put you two together so you don't have to sneak about at night. Everything is out in the open."

Alyssa blinked at the older woman while fighting panic. Nathan's mother fully expected them to have sex under her roof. The prospect both appealed and repulsed her at the same time. She waited for Nathan to protest the arrangement, but he had the nerve to thank her for understanding and then kissed Alyssa's hand. Alyssa, thinking he'd lost his damn mind, dug her nails into his palm until he winced, but he didn't release his hold.

At last, Nathan's father entered the sitting room, a proud glint in his eyes despite the stoop to his shoulders and the obvious frailty of his overall frame. Nathan popped to his feet, and Alyssa stood as well. Her heart went out to the little old man, who must have had Lydia by at least ten years. He had to be pushing seventy, or it could be the sickness that took it out of him.

"Nathan." The older man greeted Nathan with an echo of the voice of his son. "You've finally arrived. Sorry we weren't here. I forgot another doctor's appointment."

"Dad, don't worry about it." Nathan hugged his father, and Alyssa found her chest tightening. She knew the pain of losing parents without warning. Was it worse for Nathan having his dad all his life and then knowing he would go soon? Or was it easier given he could mentally prepare for the inevitable?

When the two men turned to her, she hurried over to them and allowed herself to be drawn into another hug. Whatever she had expected, it was not this warm welcome and the complete lack of reaction to her appearance. Maybe as Nathan believed, his parents just wanted to know he was happy and settling down.

"Young lady, you can call me Dad," Nathan's father insisted.

Guilt washed over Alyssa, and she stuttered.

"Dad, don't be ridiculous. They're not married or engaged!"

Alyssa turned at the voice of another person joining them. She met the caustic gaze of a woman who appeared to be a few years younger, and identified her right away as Nathan's sister. The medium-length blonde hair and blue eyes matched those of her father, a sharp contrast to Nathan's and his mother's darker looks. Her slender figure and plain clothes offered less of an impact than her mother made with obvious designer brands.

"You can call him Mr. Corde, or Leo if you don't have any respect," the woman ordered.

*Here we go.* Alyssa's hand crept to her hip almost without her guiding it there. She gave as much as she got, scraping her gaze over the woman's figure, and let it be clearly written on her face that she was not impressed with what she saw. Red stained the woman's cheeks, giving Alyssa the satisfaction she sought. "And who are you?"

"Piper Corde," was the harsh reply. "I'm Nathan's younger sister, and I can spot a gold digger from a mile away."

"Oh, is that right?" Alyssa shot back and took a step toward her. Nathan cut her off and drew her back to his side.

"Watch your mouth, Piper," he growled. "I won't allow you to talk to Alyssa that way."

"We all know it, Nathan, even if you don't. Dad and Mom were saying—"

"Piper Corde, you be quiet this instant," Lydia snapped.

A chill raised goose bumps on Alyssa's arms. So they weren't all as accepting as she'd thought. Now she remembered people loved to smile in one's face while talking behind one's back. She imagined as soon as she wasn't around, Nathan's parents would say the same thing to him that his sister wasn't too afraid to point out. She didn't doubt she would soon find herself back on a plane to the United States and the deal off. That wasn't a bad thing if Trinity held up her side of the bargain. At least she could avoid temptation in the form of Nathan Corde.

"Come on, Mom," Piper insisted, not backing down for a second. "There's only one thing someone like her wants."

Nathan opened his mouth to speak, but Alyssa held up an open palm in his face and shoved in front of him. "You know nothing about me, bitch!" She sucked in a deep breath and blew it out. "Please excuse my language, Mr. and Mrs. Corde, but I'm not going to stand here and let this *girl* think she can talk to me any kind of a way and accuse me of ensnaring Nathan for his money. You don't know my background or where I come from."

Piper looked her up and down. "Where did you buy those clothes, Wal-Mart?"

Alyssa was done talking. She sprang at Piper, who had the sense to fear for her life. Paling, she fell back a step, but before Alyssa could smack her, the barked command halted them both.

"Enough!"

The two of them turned toward Leo, and his high color and trembling hand on the top of his cane had Alyssa kicking herself for letting Piper rile her.

"I will not have this bickering in my home," Leo snapped. "My own daughter, whom I raised to be a well-mannered young woman, will not disrespect my guest. Is that clear, Piper?"

Piper's gaze lowered to the floor. "Sorry, Dad."

The argument fizzled faster than it had started, and when he'd made his point, Leo's knees gave. In the blink of an eye, both Nathan and Aziz were at his sides to catch him. Alyssa clapped a hand over her mouth. She'd vowed not to let the man suffer more than he already was, and here she stood, exacerbating his ailment.

"I'm so sorry, Mr. Corde." She followed the procession to get him seated. "Are you okay?"

The older man huffed and puffed in exhaustion. If the blood hadn't drained from his face and the bony hands didn't shake so hard, she might have thought he played up his sickness to gain control of his family. Something told her Leo Corde had commanded respect from those around him by his strength of character, not his weakness.

"I'm fine, just fine," he said, a tinge of impatience in his tone. "Call me Leo."

So he had given in to his daughter's suggestion either way. None of it mattered. She would not be here for long or in Nathan's scope after they returned to the United States. "Of course, Leo. Again, I'm sorry. If everyone will excuse me, I'd like to go to my room for a little while and get settled."

"I'll go with you," Nathan offered.

She wanted to deny him, not ready to face the fact that they would share a bed, but she couldn't do so in front of everyone else. Instead, she nodded and thanked his parents for having her once more. Nathan's touch at her lower back gave her fantasies of much more, and he led her out of the room and up the stairs. *A week will be over before I know it, and then I'm back to my own life, enjoying the success of my business. No biggie.* The time could not pass fast enough.

# Chapter Four

Alyssa made to sit down on the queen-size bed but thought better of it. Somehow that seemed to make the room smaller, bringing Nathan into proximity. As it was, she stood watching him hang a couple business suits in the closet. Didn't he ever dress down, or did he expect to work while on the island?

"I would think you'd have a maid hang up your clothes," she commented, just to have something to say.

He turned from the closet with a slight frown of concern. "I apologize. Did you need Talia to come in and help you unpack? I thought we might like some alone time to acclimate to the arrangements."

Her eyebrows went up. "Me? No, of course not. I've never been waited on in my life, aside from a waitress or whatever." When she remained silent, he decided to answer her question.

"Yes, normally, I have someone put away my things."

"Even at home?"

He smiled, and her heart skipped a beat. *Idiot heart.*

"I don't have a lot of personal time. I make the best use of it."

"That sucks." She strolled over to his suitcase and peered inside. "Tell me you have some shorts in there and a few T-shirts, maybe even some flip-flops."

"Flip-flops!" The cringe had her bursting out laughing.

"We're a couple, right, and if I'm going to pull this off realistically, I have to be myself." She stabbed his chest with a finger. "I would have bullied you into getting out of the suits. So, if you don't have anything good in there, we're going shopping, mister."

Narrowed eyes and curled lips brought her to a light pant.

"Yes, ma'am." He stepped forward, and she backed to the bed, trapped. "Don't worry. I do have shorts and T-shirts. What I'm more concerned about is if you're okay with sharing the room."

He had to go there.

"It's not what we expected, but I think we can work it out."

His gaze lit on her face. "Trust me. I won't do anything you don't want me to do, Alyssa."

She shivered hearing her name on his lips. Trust him? From what she knew of the man, he liked to keep things on the up-and-up. She had no problem trusting he wouldn't violate her. Nathan wasn't the problem. She'd been fine looking whenever in his presence, but since the beginning of this arrangement, that contentment had ebbed. His hands at her waist, his lips on hers, and the two of them writhing in bed was what filled her mind. Ridding her head of the thoughts proved impossible. Who knew if having sex with Nathan would be disgusting or unbelievably satisfying.

*You're not going to find out, Alyssa, so shut it down.*

"Stay on your side, and I'll stay on mine."

The speculative expression said the words were a poor choice. "So if I don't…"

"I'll relocate your balls with my knee."

He chuckled. "Well warned."

Alyssa might have behaved like sleeping at Nathan's side presented no big deal, but the real experience left her stiff, clutching the covers up to her neck, and listening to his quiet breathing. She'd elected to sleep in a long tee and panties, out of sight by the time he stepped from the bathroom. To her alarm, Nathan had no such qualms about revealing his body. He had slid into boxers and left his chest bare while she pretended to have drifted off. From her side of the bed, she took in the fresh scent of soap and sexy maleness every time she inhaled. Sleep eluded her, but Nathan didn't appear to have an issue.

Frustrated, she rolled to her side facing Nathan and stared at the broad expanse of his back. A sense of longing came over her to reach out and touch. Before she knew what she was doing, her fingers brushed the warm skin, and she gasped.

"I thought we agreed to stay on our own sides."

She jumped at his voice. "You were pretending to be asleep."

"And you weren't earlier?"

41

"Whatever."

He shifted to face her, and she did her best to keep her eyes on his face and not the smooth, hairless chest. Did he shave it, or was it naturally that way? She licked her lips and was gratified to find him focusing on the movement in the dim lighting. *No, you're not trying to turn him on, Alyssa. Go to sleep.*

The mattress creaked when he moved closer to her, sinking under his heavy weight. She tumbled nearer without meaning to and rested her palms on his chest. Tingles brought goose bumps to her arms when his hand landed at her waist. She might as well be naked for all the protection the tee provided against his burning touch.

"We didn't agree to this," she informed him.

"You started it."

Despite herself she chuckled. "I don't know why I can't imagine a big-time executive like you teasing me like a little kid."

He lowered his head, bringing his mouth into proximity with hers. "I do more than tease."

"Meaning I don't?" *Okay, seriously, girl, don't challenge the man.*

"Prove me wrong."

"I'm not falling for that, pal."

His gaze dropped to her hands, still resting against his warm skin. With effort, she removed them and curled her fingers into her palms to keep from going back.

"We don't have to deny ourselves, Alyssa."

Why the heck did he have to keep speaking her name in that sexy deep tone?

No doubt oblivious to her torment, he continued. "We're adults. We can explore what's before us."

Her stomach muscles tautened. "What's before us?"

"Attraction. You're a beautiful woman, and from the way you're looking at me as if I'm your next meal—"

"I am *not* looking at you like I want to eat you! Wow, somebody's full of themselves." While she protested, she bit down on a laugh. He'd spoken the truth, and there had been no arrogance, just an observation. If she said, *"Let's get it on,"* he would comply. After all, Nathan didn't worry about falling in deeper than he intended. Not from what she saw anyway. She bit her lip. "Don't you feel weird having sex in your mother's house?"

"Not the first time."

She glared at him, and he smiled.

"Teenage hormones."

She rolled her eyes, attempting to give the impression she didn't give a damn about his past, but he squashed her act with one touch of his fingertip. From her cheek to her lips, he traced a path. She turned her head.

"You shouldn't do that."

"Give me one reason why I shouldn't."

"Because."

He raised his eyebrows. She fought not to turn her head back so her lips would graze his palm. He would not be put off, but squeezed her hip where his other hand lay. His thigh brushed hers, and she tensed against the hardness of his muscles. Just feeling that little bit led her to thinking about what lay above and between his legs. Was he hard there too? *Don't even, Alyssa.*

43

"I think it would be a bad idea to complicate matters." She lowered her gaze from his face so he wouldn't see the desire bubbling inside. "I don't jump into bed with men I hardly know. Not that I'm judging you…"

"Of course not," he teased.

All of a sudden, the space between them compressed even more, although she didn't see him move. His breath warmed her lips, recalling how good it felt to kiss him. One wouldn't hurt, would it? She could taste him and enjoy it, then roll over and go to sleep. Shocked at the sharp turn to her thoughts, she jerked away from him and flipped over. Nathan's hand rose as she spun, but it settled in place the moment she stilled.

"If I tell you to move that…"

"I will," he assured her.

She chewed some more on her lip. Damn the man for making her want him. She drew her knees up and squeezed her eyes shut. No amount of deep breathing and willing her mind would make her relax.

"Wound that tight, you'll never rest. Here, let me help you," he offered.

"I know what kind of help you want to give me."

He slid in close and spooned her. She clenched her jaw and bit off a squeak of alarm. Now she knew, the hardness extended to his member. The shaft jutted against her ass as he folded himself around her, but he made no move to do any more than hold her. His embrace tightened with an arm slung over her waist and a palm splayed across her belly. The other arm he lay on the pillow above her head. On one hand, he heightened her desires, but his nearness

44

evoked peace as well. In degrees, she began to settle down.

She thought he kissed her hair, but decided it had to be a figment of her imagination. How had they gotten to this point, to be comfortable enough with each other that they could lie in bed together as if they were a real couple? Would it have gone the same way if Trinity were here instead? Maybe her cousin would have taken everything in stride, or then again, Nathan might have respected Trinity's love of her boyfriend and kept his distance in private. Alyssa, as a single woman, was fair game.

With these thoughts, that any available woman would do to satisfy his lust, she managed to cool her horny body and fell into a fitful sleep, and by the time she woke up in the morning with sunlight streaming into the room, Nathan was nowhere in sight. She rose and showered, then found a sundress to wear to breakfast. Now the challenge would begin.

In the dining room, Nathan's family was seated around the table. Annoyance rose in her a little that no one had waited for her. Nathan stood the moment he spotted her and strode around the table dressed in a business suit. Without thinking, she frowned at him.

"I thought you said you were going to dress down while we're here." She gasped after she blurted the words and started to apologize. He cut her off with a kiss that took the strength from her knees and forced her to cling to the lapels of his jacket. The fool had the nerve to appear pleased, which pissed her off even more.

"Good morning, my love. I'm sorry. I did promise you, but I have an unexpected meeting. The second it's over, I will be at your disposal to dress me as you see fit—or *un*dress."

Piper gagged. "Keep that in your room! The least you can do is say good morning. Maybe they don't teach you manners where you're from."

Nathan's eyes blazed in anger, but Alyssa squeezed his arm. "I apologize, Mr. and Mrs. Corde. Leo and Lydia. Good morning. I hope you two had a good night's sleep?"

Alyssa chose the spot next to where Nathan sat, and he held her chair for her. She made no effort to greet his bitchy sister whatsoever, even while the woman stared daggers at her.

Lydia was the first to speak up. "Good morning, sweetheart. I'm sorry we started without you. I wanted Nathan to wake you, but he said you didn't sleep much last night and to let you rest." The insinuation came through crystal clear, and Alyssa couldn't help blushing.

"No problem." Alyssa spotted the food on trays on a side table and started to get up to serve herself, but Nathan rested a hand on her thigh. Arrows of desire pinged her pussy, and she turned slightly to get him to let go. He ignored her fidgeting to whisper in her ear.

"Just tell Talia what you'd like."

She glanced up to find the maid standing at her elbow. *Goodness, they move like ghosts, flitting in and out.* "Um eggs, bacon, and a biscuit, please, Talia. Thanks."

"Of course, miss."

The others seemed not to be fazed in the least to be served in their own home as Aziz and Talia moved about the table refreshing coffee, bringing second helpings. The food sat not even five feet away from them. In fact, the table extended wide enough to have placed the dishes in the middle.

"I have an idea," Lydia announced. "Why don't us girls go shopping? You and I can keep Alyssa company, Piper, while Nathan's working. How's that sound?"

Alyssa dredged up a smile, and Piper whirled a finger in the air, but she didn't refuse to go. In fact, from the determined set to her jaw, Alyssa wouldn't be surprised if she had a verbal attack coming. Well, she could bring it, because Alyssa did not take crap from anyone. She knew she was a decent person, and she had no plans to try to swindle Nathan out of his money. Besides, who could think of money when a man like him kissed the way he did? She squirmed in her chair once more and was rewarded with another squeeze from the man himself. He would get his own lecture later about going too far!

# Chapter Five

At the front door, where Nathan had insisted she accompany him out of sight of the others, he pulled his wallet from his pocket and flipped it open. She shrank back. "What are you doing?"

He thumbed through a thick stack of money. "I don't have much cash on me."

She folded her arms over her chest. "I don't want it."

He forced her to extend her palm and dropped several hundreds into it. Alyssa's mouth went dry when she counted out two thousand, but he wasn't done. A credit card topped the stack. "Use this if you need more, and if they give you any issues, call me. I'll clear it."

Her jaw went slack. "Nathan, I do not need this money, and even if I did, it's too much."

He curled her fingers closed. She couldn't help getting caught up in his gaze, mesmerized by their depth and warmth. "You are going shopping with my mom and sister.

They love to buy things, and the stores they frequent aren't…"

She frowned. "Wal-Mart?"

"They're exclusive. That cash probably won't be enough. Spend as much as you want. There's no limit on the card."

"No limit?" She blinked at him. The last credit card she owned had a limit of five hundred dollars, and she'd maxed it out countless times before learning discipline to go with cash or don't buy. She would not go backward by using his card.

"Wouldn't my family expect me to be generous with the woman I love?" he argued.

"I know, but—"

"You would fight me, but I assure you, I would not give up until you allowed me to take care of you in the way that I can. So, let's skip all of that and go straight to you accepting the money."

"Nathan!"

His serene smile made her sigh to keep from smacking him.

"Fine, but I'll use the money, not the card. I'll consider it expenses while on the job."

"Good girl." He patted her ass and kissed her lips and then was gone before she could tell him about himself.

Alyssa turned on her heel and headed to her room to freshen up a little before the shopping spree with his mom and sister. Nathan Corde was used to getting his way, but before the week ended, she would set him straight. Every woman did not fall for his charm, least of all her.

An hour later, she, Lydia, and Piper were whisked into the city by yet another employee of their household, the chauffeur. When Lydia started mentioning names like Dolce & Gabbana, she knew the two thousand would not cover a sock, let alone the dresses the older woman chattered about wanting to buy.

"What do you think of this dress?" Lydia suggested, holding up a strawberry-print piece that included the bright red fruit, butterflies, and flowers. Alyssa held her physical reaction in check and smiled, reaching for the dress.

"That's nice." She took a peek at the price tag and stood corrected. She could buy more than a sock. This D&G dress was just thirteen hundred dollars. Her mouth went dry reading the numbers, and she marveled over the fact that Lydia hadn't blinked twice at it. Correction again. Lydia never even looked at the tag. She didn't need to.

In her excitement, the older woman wandered off along the aisle, and Alyssa started after her, but Piper blocked her path. "For what it's worth, she meant that dress for herself, not you. Mom loves flower patterns. The more colorful, the better."

Alyssa softened. "Thanks. Whew, I didn't know how I was going to tell her it's not my style."

Piper cocked her head to the side and sneered. "Not just the style, huh? I bet that cost more than you make in a month."

"And what? I'm supposed to be ashamed of what I make just because you're rich? Please, don't even worry about me losing sleep over what you can afford versus what I can."

"I'm sure you don't. Lose sleep, I mean."

Alyssa gritted her teeth. She shoved the dress at Piper. "You have two seconds to get out of my face."

"Or?" Thin, shaped eyebrows rose.

She was right, of course. Hitting the bitch would ruin everything, but that didn't mean she had to bite her tongue. Alyssa leaned her weight into one leg and put her hand on her hip. She mugged Piper from her red polished toes, peeking out through high-heeled sandals, to her long silken tresses. "Even if I pay five dollars for a dress, I'd look a hell of a lot better in it than any designer piece you drape on your skinny ass."

With those words, Alyssa ran a hand over her curves and smacked her round booty. To her satisfaction, Piper's cheeks puffed out, and her color turned crimson, giving her the appearance of a tomato. Alyssa chuckled and moved past her to find Lydia.

The two of them traded insults for much of the day in between Alyssa trying to spend as little money as possible. Frustrated with the prohibitive price tags, she suggested a middle-class store, and was surprised but gratified when Lydia agreed. She managed to purchase a dress and a couple of shorts sets, a pair of flip-flops with fake bling that were cute, and a few hair bands to keep her unruly hair in order. The fact that Piper behaved as if she might catch a disease just mingling with those of lesser fortune provided greater satisfaction. Lydia's happy bounce never wavered.

"Okay, I don't know about you ladies, but I'm starving," Lydia announced at one. "Let's find somewhere to eat."

"Sounds good," Alyssa agreed, and Piper echoed the assent.

The same restaurant she and Nathan attended the day before turned out to be the choice, and to Alyssa's delight, the host bustled up, and after greeting Lydia and Piper by name, he turned to her with a warm smile. "Ms. Alyssa, good to see you again."

"Jeff, hello. Thank you, same to you," she answered.

Lydia nodded as if the situation was as it should be, but Piper glared. Alyssa glided past her, head held high, as Jeff led them to the private room. She had scarcely put in her order before her phone rang, and she read Nathan's name on the screen. She slid her chair back. "Excuse me a moment, please."

She left the room and strolled a little along the hall and around a corner. When she pressed the connect button, the sound of Nathan's voice echoing across the lines brought her body to life and activated her imagination of his handsome face.

"Hey," she breathed.

"Alyssa, everything going okay?"

She wanted to forbid him from saying her name. One would think she'd never been attracted to a man. "Yes, everything is fine. I actually had fun with your mother. She's a shopaholic, but she was a good sport to go with me to the regular stores."

"Regular stores?"

"Never mind. Work going fine?"

"Yes, I'm finished for now. I had a local businessman contact me a few months ago about a possible venture here in the islands, and when he heard I'd come down, he requested a meeting. I promise I won't let it get in the way of us."

She pushed a trembling hand through her hair. "Well, this isn't real, right, so no biggie."

"I want it to be as real as possible."

She would not rise to that bait. "Do you want me to come back? We've just sat down to lunch. If you're close, you can join us. We're at the same place you took me last night."

"I am close." Why did his voice drop as if he sought to seduce her? "I look forward to seeing you. Please ask the waiter to bring my usual. I'll be twenty minutes at the longest."

Alyssa shifted from one foot to the other, trying to calm her idiot body. "O-Okay, sure."

"See you then."

He hung up, and she breathed a sigh of relief. Then the thought of him arriving so soon hit her, and anticipation took over. He would no doubt greet her with a kiss, and a hand at her waist or back. Longing turned her around to the point that she walked in the opposite direction to where she intended. She started back the way she came and then stopped at a familiar voice coming from behind a door to her left. Maybe this was the room and she'd forgotten. Shaking her head in confusion, she pushed at the panels, glad it wasn't shut all the way.

Piper came into view and then a woman she didn't recognize. "I told you I would call you," Piper said to the woman, who had dark hair cropped so close to her head, she seemed more like a soft-featured man than a woman. Her figure, almost as slender as Piper's was unmistakably female, though, with large breasts and curvy hips.

The woman frowned and drew Piper close, so close that their chests touched. Alyssa expected Piper to jerk away, but she stayed in the embrace and lowered her lashes like a woman in the throes of desire.

"Why wouldn't I try to see you?" the woman complained. "I hate that you haven't told them about me yet. It's been three years, Piper. I think it's time, and I got my dad to agree to let me come down here. Please, just—"

"No. Look, I love you, but I'm not ready."

Alyssa didn't realize she'd gasped until the two women turned in her direction. All the blood drained from Piper's face, and she rocked so much on her feet, her girlfriend had to steady her. Alyssa took a step back.

"Um, sorry, I think I have the wrong room." She yanked the door shut with too much force and spun on her heel. In seconds, she arrived back at her seat and dropped into it, panting.

Lydia frowned in concern. "Are you okay, sweetheart?"

Alyssa forced a smile. "I'm fine, thanks." She scrambled for an excuse while trying to make sense of what she'd just witnessed. "Oh, Nathan is going to join us for lunch, so I need to order him something."

Lydia clapped her hands. "Good! We can show him what we bought. Leo gets worn out too quickly, so I have to make Nathan endure it." She laughed. "He's a good son. He doesn't complain."

Alyssa laughed. "So you know what you're doing."

The older woman winked. "Of course. Men are here to serve us, darling. Never forget that."

"Yes, ma'am."

They continued to chat after Alyssa put in Nathan's order with the waiter, and just before he arrived, Piper returned to the table alone. She sat down, more subdued than Alyssa had seen her since they met, and the younger woman refused to meet her gaze. With her hands in her lap, Piper's shoulders remained high and stiff. The moment her brother arrived, the tension in them grew still more. Alyssa guessed she waited on pins and needles for Alyssa to blow her cover.

*If I was the bitch she thinks I am, I'd have her. Maybe now she'll get off my back when she realizes I don't give a damn about her secrets.*

"Mom, Piper," Nathan greeted his family and then leaned over to kiss Alyssa. She offered him her cheek, but a click of his tongue in chastisement made her raise her chin, and he kissed her lips. He took the seat next to her and scooted closer to Alyssa's side, as if he weren't near enough. She did her best not to fidget, but Nathan seemed at ease, damn the man. "So, ladies, how did the shopping go?"

Lydia launched into a play-by-play of everywhere they'd gone and everything they'd said while there. Between sips of wine, she rifled through bags to pull out items to show her son. Alyssa wondered how she could go on with so few breaths at her age. All the while, Nathan's expression of polite interest never changed. On impulse, Alyssa laid a hand on his thigh, and the muscles tautened under her touch. She jerked away, but Nathan caught her fingers and placed them back on his leg. He peered down at her, causing her heartbeat to increase.

"Okay?" he whispered.

"Of course," she murmured back.

Across the table, Piper knocked over a glass of water, and a waiter materialized from nowhere to mop up the mess. Nathan studied his sister in silence. Her hands fluttered all the more, and the same server saved the replacement glass from her destruction just in time.

"Is there something bothering you, Piper?" Nathan queried.

"Why should it be?" she croaked and then cleared her throat. "I'm fine. Worry about your girlfriend."

Nathan looked from his sister to Alyssa and back again. Alyssa rolled her eyes and shrugged.

"They think I don't know, but the two of them haven't been getting along all morning," Lydia said. "I'm trying to stay positive, but I don't like the negativity. It's not good for Dad."

All conversation came to a halt. Guilt tightened the muscles in Alyssa's chest. She'd thought Lydia's constant chatter the result of just her personality, but from her words, she realized she worried about her husband.

"I'm sorry, Mom." Piper's sincerity shone clear in her watery gaze. That they each felt the pain of Leo's sickness no matter the happy face they put on brought home to Alyssa that she didn't belong among them, least of all at a time like this. She considered informing Nathan when they were alone that she would fly home tomorrow. He could say she'd had an emergency.

"I'm not very hungry," Lydia announced.

The food arrived, and with the assistance of a couple servers was soon in place on the table. Nathan pulled his wallet from his back pocket. "I'm afraid we won't be able to stay. This should cover everything." He tossed a few bills on the table, and Alyssa guessed it amounted to much more than the charge plus a generous tip.

The waiter's brows rose. "I apologize, Mr. Corde. Was there something you weren't satisfied with in our service or the food?"

"Not at all. A family matter."

"Of course, sir. Shall we box this up?"

Nathan rose. "That won't be necessary."

Alyssa shook her head. "Oh hell no, we can't just waste food like this. Please, box it all. We can eat it later if we get hungry, or for dinner. Thanks."

All three Cordes looked at her like she'd lost her mind. Alyssa crossed her arms and stared back. Amusement brightened Nathan's eyes, and he ran a hand down her arm. "You heard the woman. Please box everything."

As they left the restaurant, Alyssa expected backlash from Piper but got nothing. The woman took the seat opposite her in the limo and stared out the window. Alyssa sat at Nathan's side, and he grasped her hand in his, lacing his fingers with hers. His mother took the seat beside Piper, and soon they arrived at the mansion.

When the car door opened at the chauffeur's guidance, she started to get out, but Nathan held her back. She glanced up at him, but he said nothing while his mother and sister vacated the vehicle. When they had gone inside, he waved the driver away.

"Give us a moment, Felix."

The man nodded and shut the door. Wary, Alyssa faced Nathan. "What's up?"

He hesitated and then patted her hand. Something told her she wouldn't like what was coming.

"We don't…usually box food we don't eat."

She tilted her head to the side, studying him. "And what? Oh, did I embarrass you?"

"Not embarrass exactly. You don't know how we do things."

Alyssa looked away from him and tugged her hand free of his. She raised it to gesture while she spoke, thought better of the words she intended, and tapped a finger across her lips.

"I don't know how you do things?" For the life of her, she couldn't get a grip on the rising anger. "So in other words, you waste food on a regular basis, un*touched* food, food that was slaved over in a hot kitchen for you, food that could have gone to someone else who would appreciate it, but instead, they had to be ousted because your family showed up unannounced at a restaurant where they require reservations."

Nathan drew back as if she'd slapped him. The displeasure radiated off of him. "It's not a situation we need to argue about, Alyssa. We just need to come to an agreement that—"

"Oh, an agreement!"

His eyebrows snapped together over darkened eyes. "Alyssa."

"Don't Alyssa me." He had no idea of the many nights she had to do with ramen and green beans because she couldn't afford meat when money got tight. That wasn't his fault, but the man knew nothing of suffering, and she wouldn't sit here and be made to feel ashamed of asking for a box.

He sighed, a long-suffering sound that pissed her off all the more.

"I'm not angry. Nor am I scolding you as if you'd made a mistake. I respect who you are and your experiences."

"Yeah, I'll just bet you do."

He grabbed for her hand, but she moved it out of reach. Not to be put off, he slid a palm over her belly, and she could have cussed out her own flesh at the reaction of his touch. Short of fleeing the car, she sat stuck.

"Contrary to your assumptions, we do not make a habit of wasting food."

"But you don't eat leftovers. I don't even know why we're sitting here having this discussion. It's pointless. Okay, I won't ask for anything to be boxed again. Happy?"

He stroked her cheek, and his face softened. "How about we offer the food to the staff? Will that make you happy?"

*As if he's really my man and needs to make me happy.* "Okay. That sounds good."

"Great. Shall we go inside?"

He opened the door and gestured for her to precede him into the house. Alyssa wondered what else she'd have to learn about rich people and how their worlds did not mesh before the end of her foray into fantasyland ended.

# Chapter Six

"Our turn," Nathan announced and stood to pull Alyssa from her seat. She followed him to the middle of the floor and glanced over to his dad and mom, sitting side by side, with Piper sitting nearby in a recliner, bare feet drawn up to her chest. Alyssa could not believe they were playing charades, but she had to admit it was fun. Leo didn't participate, but enjoyed laughing at their antics. Alyssa, who didn't get out to social gatherings that much where she might have learned better skills at these types of games, sucked royal ass at it and despised whoever had suggested the entertainment. Then again, it might have been Nathan, and she glared at him. She speculated on whether he'd suggested the game because he thought it was something she as a middle-class woman would enjoy. On another thought, the three Cordes were decent at picking up each other's clues, while she missed most.

"You can do this, honey," he encouraged her. "Just remember tugging of the ear means 'sounds like.' If I hold up fingers, it indicates the number of words, or if we're down to a single word, number of syllables."

She grumbled at him, "I remember that part."

"I can't believe you haven't played this more than once in your life, darling," Lydia said, making her feel worse.

Alyssa stabbed an accusing finger toward her pretend boyfriend. "Nathan's acting stinks. I need a better partner, that's all."

"You will pay for that remark, woman."

"Gag," was Piper's single comment.

Nathan took the hat from his father's hands. "It's your turn to act it out, Alyssa, so make it good."

The game continued, and Alyssa found out it wasn't Nathan's impressions of scenes and words that presented the problem. They soon had to admit defeat, and Lydia, gracious hostess that she was, offered the best player to pair with Alyssa for the next round—Piper. Nathan's younger sister popped up from her chair and strode with purpose over to Alyssa. She all but dragged her toward the door, calling over her shoulder, "Quick strategy session," and the others, including Leo, burst out laughing.

The second the door clicked closed behind them, Piper dropped her hold on Alyssa's arm. The woman's entire visage transformed into one of dislike and suspicion. "What are you waiting for?"

"Excuse me?"

Piper lowered her voice. "You heard me. What are you waiting for? We both know what you saw back at the restaurant, so why haven't you told my family? I thought that's why you kept Nathan talking in the car after Mom and I got out, but he didn't say anything to me or act like he knew my secret."

Alyssa rocked back on her heels and folded her arms over her chest. "It must have killed you waiting for us to come inside, huh?"

"Don't play games with me, bitch."

Alyssa laughed. "Go ahead. Please get in my face. I dare you."

Piper seemed to think better of stepping to Alyssa, and she took a couple steps in retreat. "I get it. You want to hold it over my head a while, waiting for the right time, when it benefits you the most."

"Wow, is this how you all are? Trusting no one, assuming the worst?" Alyssa shook her head and turned toward the living room, her hand on the knob. "I don't give two figs about what you do with your personal life. If you haven't come out to your family, that's your problem. If you think I'm lying and that I'm just waiting for the right time, I don't give a crap about that either. Stay in the hall sulking like an infant if you want to. I'm going in."

Alyssa put on a smile and rubbed her hands together as if she had the greatest plan in the world to overthrow Nathan and his mom. "Ready, you two? You're going down. Just want you to know this."

Nathan cast her a curious glance, but then smiled in return. "Not on your life, baby. You're beautiful, but I have to show you who has the upper hand."

"Aw, that's the sweetest thing to say," Lydia purred.

"My boy," Leo echoed.

Alyssa rolled her eyes. "How was that sweet? The man wants to control me. You don't know who you're dealing with, Mr. Nathan Corde."

A challenge reflected in the hazel eyes locked with hers. "I'm beginning to find out, and I think I will continue."

The game progressed, and a short while later, Alyssa whooped in triumph. "See, I told you! We schooled you, Nathan and Lydia."

"Yes, you did school us, dear," Lydia admitted.

Alyssa burst out laughing at the woman's use of slang. Nathan conceded defeat with less aplomb. She stuck her tongue out at him, and he nabbed her before she could scurry away. He captured her chin and lowered his head as if to kiss her, when Lydia cried out.

"Leo, are you okay?" The terror in those high-pitched words tore across Alyssa's chest. Nathan released her and spun on his heel to his father.

"Dad?"

All three Cordes bent over Leo, who had paled more than he already was. His hands shook with violence, and he seemed to have trouble catching his breath. Nathan's gaze bore into hers. "Get Aziz now!"

Alyssa nodded and fled the room, shouting for the butler. As Nathan carried his father to the car, Aziz screeched to a halt at the front of the house. Alyssa realized Felix did not live in the house like the other two did, nor did the cook and the assistant maid who helped Talia during the day. Aziz would drive.

Alyssa hung back as the others piled into the car, and Nathan took her hand after he'd buckled his father inside. "Get in," he commanded. She didn't protest when his grip tightened to the point of pain. The set of his jaw, the pallor of his own skin, and the way he never looked at her but didn't take his gaze off his father displayed his fear. He loved his dad, and this situation bore heavy on him.

She settled in at his side as they whisked to the hospital. Lydia barked sharp orders into her cell phone while holding Leo's hand. By the time they drew into the driveway at the emergency entrance, orderlies were wheeling a gurney toward them, and a man who must have been a doctor by his authoritative presence stood nearby.

The next hour dragged by with the family in the waiting room and Lydia in with Leo. Nathan paced, and Piper sat with feet drawn up, shivering in her chair. The blank expression in her eyes told Alyssa she didn't realize she'd left the house without her shoes. Alyssa stood and walked over to the triage station. "Any way we can get some of those socks with the nonskid stuff on the bottom?"

The nurse opened her mouth as if to say no. Alyssa interrupted. "The Cordes are so worried about their dad, Piper forgot her shoes."

"The Cordes, oh yes, of course."

Alyssa bit down on the bitterness and thanked the woman for the socks. She handed them to Piper, who sat staring at them in her hand. Nathan stooped in front of her and drew them onto her feet. Piper muttered her thanks to her brother, and Alyssa returned to her chair. Time crawled by. Nathan returned to her side and cupped her face between two hands before resting his forehead against hers. "Thank you for being here."

"You don't need me," she whispered back and struggled with the ache caused from seeing his pain. "You're surrounded by your family, and that's what's important. It might be best if Aziz takes me back to your house."

"Stay…please."

He gave no elaboration, and she nodded in silence. They sat side by side waiting, and at last, Lydia appeared, looking haggard. The change in the stylish woman worried Alyssa all the more. "He's out of the woods for now. They say we can see him, but not too long. They're moving him to the ICU, and I'm staying the night."

Nathan drew his mother into his arms, and she allowed herself a quick cry before forcing a smile. Alyssa didn't know how she did it. This time when Nathan tried bringing her along, she dug her heels in and remained in the waiting room until they returned. Just as Lydia indicated, the visit lasted no more than a few moments. Then they were on their way back to the mansion. The silent interior of the car weighed down, and Alyssa hopped out of the vehicle the second it came to a complete stop. She checked her watch and noted the late hour. A glance at Nathan showed he wasn't ready to sleep.

"Good night," Piper murmured and headed up to the stairs. If her brother's response reached her ears, Alyssa would have been surprised. She took his arm and tugged him in the direction of the kitchen.

"This way," she told him. He hesitated, a questioning expression spreading over his face. "Comfort food."

They strode into the kitchen, which Alyssa had so far only glimpsed in passing. The room expanded bigger than her apartment. Nathan dropped into a chair and leaned back in it. The faraway look in his eyes told her he moved on automatic.

Shoving aside the fact that she was a guest, Alyssa raided the refrigerator. As she expected, a chocolate cake sat on one shelf with a single slice missing. Good. She wouldn't need to feel bad about cutting into a brand-new one. After she'd arranged a piece for her and a piece for Nathan in bowls, she discovered vanilla ice cream in the freezer and heaped two spoonfuls for each of them into the dishes.

"Eat," she commanded, sitting across from Nathan. "The sugar will give you a boost—artificial and short term, but every little bit helps."

Nathan moved mechanically and spooned cake and ice cream into his mouth. After a few bites, his gaze rose to hers. "How did you know about this?"

She laughed. "A few broken hearts."

"Ah."

The sweet, creamy dessert eased down her throat, an old friend always willing to be there. *Except when I hate her because she made me gain weight. Then she can kiss my ass.* "Yup, women really do this. It's not just for the movies. You have to have seen Piper eat—" Maybe he hadn't. Not that his sister couldn't get a broken heart, but she guessed Piper kept even that a secret because of her preference.

"No, I haven't," he confirmed.

"Lucky you. The tears and snot accompany it, and that's so not pretty."

67

He cringed and put his spoon down.

"Damn, I'm sorry. I didn't mean to kill your appetite."

"You didn't. I was just thinking how great you are. This is just a gig, I guess you can call it, and you're all in. You helped me, and even Piper when she needed it. I just wanted to say thank you." He reached across the table and touched her fingers. She wanted to draw back, to protect herself, but the haunted light had returned to his eyes.

"You all love him very much. I can tell."

"You have no idea."

Nathan ran his hands through his hair and stood. He paced a few steps away from the table and leaned on the island in the middle of the kitchen. The stove was situated there, one with five burners and a rack overhead, pots and pans hanging from it. Alyssa had always wanted something like that. Her apartment stove looked like someone had squished it between the sink and the refrigerator. The burners were so tight, she had trouble getting food prepared in a big soup pot to cook evenly.

"When I was younger, he was stronger and tougher. He didn't allow failure in his subordinates or his family. That doesn't mean he was a tyrant. His kindness reached every corner of the world, and no matter how busy running a corporation made him, he found time to spend with Piper and me."

Alyssa had never heard anyone who wasn't a child idolize their parent so much. She admired it in Nathan.

"I strove to be like him in every way."

"I bet you did."

He turned to look at her and offered a tight smile. "Not

even close. Like any son, I thought he would be here forever. Losing him will be unbearable."

Alyssa's spoon clanked in her bowl when she let it fall, and she rushed over to Nathan. He engulfed her in a bone-crushing hug. She held on, willing her strength to him, but when she peered up, his eyes were dry. He lowered his head toward hers, and his lashes brushed her cheeks. He pulled in a deep breath, his big chest pushing against hers.

"It's late," he murmured.

She kissed his cheek and drew from his arms. After they'd washed and dried the dishes they had used, they walked up to the bedroom they shared. Alyssa showered and slipped into a nightgown she'd purchased shopping. Then she climbed into bed. Nathan took longer in the bathroom, but when he returned, he appeared no more unwound than before he went in. She considered offering to find Talia for a sleeping pill, but had another thought.

Nathan climbed into bed and switched off the lamp. The bed sank toward his side, bringing her in closer to him. He lay on his back, and she rested a hand on his bare chest.

"Nathan."

"Hm."

"I...um..." Rather than ask him or offer, she ran her hand over his chest, skimmed his nipples, and then explored lower, across his belly. Just before she reached the point of no return, he caught her wrist. She eyed him in the dim lighting. Was he rejecting her?

"I don't want to take advantage of you."

"You're not."

"If you weren't feeling sorry for me, you wouldn't offer this."

She sucked her teeth. "We both know that's not true. We felt it from day one. I'm a big girl."

"Alyssa." He rolled to face her, continuing to hold her wrist in the spot where he'd stopped it. "I'm not in a position to think clearly. I want to forget my head altogether. That might not be the best choice for you."

She stretched up and nibbled his bottom lip. The sharp intake of breath brought his chest to her pebbled nipples, and the thin nightgown material did nothing to disguise her state. In a moment, she figured Nathan would not be able to turn back. With the tip of her tongue, she teased the soft skin at his mouth and dared to dip inside to the warm moistness. A low groan rumbled in his throat.

His arm shot out to encircle her waist, and he hauled her tight to his chest. Already, his cock had grown hard behind his boxers. Alyssa ran a toe up his leg and down again. He shuddered. When she raised it once more, he caught her behind the knee to keep her legs spread. Her pussy clenched in anticipation.

He parted her lips with his tongue and covered her mouth with such force, it took her breath away. She surrendered to his hungry kiss and knotted her fingers in his hair.

After a few moments, he drew away. "I don't want you to regret this in the morning."

"I won't." She tilted her head back when he tasted her at her throat.

"Take if off."

She swallowed and leaned back to pull the nightgown over her head. Lying flat, arms up, she let him study her body in the pale moonlight. Did he like what he saw? Her breasts were still firm at thirty-three, but not as high as they were ten years ago. She thought the size wasn't bad, not too small, but not Dolly either.

Nathan's fingers splayed over her rib cage, and his thumb found her nipple to pluck at it. The caress sent signals to her nether regions, making her wetter.

"You're so beautiful." He kissed her lips before she could answer and then traced down her chest, leaving small pecks along the way. When his lips closed over the very nipple he'd been playing with, her back came up off the bed. She keened in need. The noises he made with his mouth when he reached her navel drove her insane. He raised his head. "Are you okay with me going down here?"

"Are you serious?"

Nathan thrust the covers away and boosted her thighs. He scooted farther down the bed, and she couldn't help the shudder that rocked her from head to toe. A curse rose to her lips the second his mouth closed over her clit. What was she thinking? This man—holding out against him meant nothing. She would give it all. His kiss, his touch, his body would demand surrender, if not his words.

"Nathan," she moaned.

Speaking his name seemed to spur him on. He sucked harder at her bud, and she bit off a scream. Come dripped down from between her folds. She felt it, and he didn't let it go to waste. Holding her knees in a firm grip, he shoved her legs higher and began licking at her cream. The sensation of his tongue delving inside, retracting to swallow, and then going in again had her squirming. Just when she thought the pleasure bearable, he took it up a notch by returning to her clit again. First flicking it with his tongue, he switched to sucking it between his lips. The abuse of the poor bud demanded she release, and her body geared toward climax. Inner muscles contracting, Alyssa tangled fingers in Nathan's hair and pumped his face.

"Mm, yes, yes, yes. Make me come. Make me come!"

He didn't let up, but worked her clit until the orgasm slammed through her core and spread outward. She screamed his name, forgetting there were others in the house. Again and again, she rode his face, until her satisfaction was complete.

Nathan leaped from the bed and shed his boxers. He rustled through the wallet he'd tossed on the dresser earlier and found a condom. Within moments, he sheathed his tool and climbed onto the bed. She was about to raise her legs again, but he tugged an ankle.

"No, turn over. On your knees."

She obeyed, hiking her ass in the air. Nathan locked strong fingers on her hips. Her mouth went dry at the first touch of his cock head. A mewl of need rose in her throat, and Nathan echoed the sound with his own growl. Soon the cap pierced her opening. She whimpered his name.

"Alyssa, oh hell, you're so wonderfully tight. Even after you've come. Baby, you feel incredible."

He seated himself deep inside her, and her heart palpitated. She licked her lips and braced with one hand on the headboard. "Give it to me."

His fingers spasmed at her hips, and he withdrew only to grind to the hilt, a violent and amazing movement. She arched her back as much as she could and shoved into him. He filled her to capacity, her walls seeming to stretch around the biggest dick she'd ever enjoyed. *More. I have to have more.*

"Make me come again like this, Nathan. *Please.*"

He ground in and out at a steady pace and then reached under her with long fingers to her clit. Rather than stroke it, he squeezed the sensitive flesh between his digits while pounding against her ass. Words, rational thought, anything that had nothing to do with living on the end of Nathan's cock, left her. All she did was feel his thrusts and hear his ragged breathing. He stimulated her with dirty phrases and occasional smacks on her ass. Nathan's ability to hold off his release surprised her, and just when she reached her second peak, he drove into her wet pussy once more and held still. A powerful orgasm exploded over her being, and following on its heels, Nathan found his own climax.

Her lover wrapped both arms around her waist, and keeping himself buried inside her, he dragged her down to the bed so that he spooned her. They lay still for long moments, both panting. After a while, he pulled out, and Alyssa heard the slap of the condom coming off. She kept her eyes closed. He moved away, and she mourned his loss, but he returned quickly. She twisted in his arms and rested on his chest. He held her tight to him. A huge yawn expanded his chest, and she sighed in satisfaction.

"You want to do it again?"

She opened her eyes and stared up at him. "Are you serious?"

"Yes, you don't want to?"

She grinned. "I'm in."

# Chapter Seven

Alyssa woke and stretched, sore in every muscle in her body. She expected to find herself alone, but Nathan lay at her side, asleep. She rolled over and watched him. His lashes were long and thick for a man. They swept his cheeks, making him appear so sweet in repose. Did he ever get angry or raise his voice? Was he the kind of man who cheated on a woman or lied to her? All she'd seen so far was his deep love of his dad, a bit of his kindness, and a touch of sadness, which he hid most of all. What gave him genuine joy or made him burst out laughing with total abandon?

*All right, girl. You're getting carried away. It doesn't matter. He's not yours, and you're not going to learn any more about him.* Certainly not in a week.

Someone knocked at the door, and she started. Nathan woke in an instant and tugged the sheets up over her naked figure. She marveled that he was aware of her and her state of dress so soon after being jarred awake.

"Nathan," Piper called through the door. "Are you going with me to the hospital?"

He sat up and ran a hand through his disordered hair. Alyssa bit her lip. Even with bedhead, sexiness oozed from his pores. No doubt a string of broken hearts lay in this man's wake.

"Come in," he called, and she opened the door fully dressed. The frown she tossed in Alyssa's direction made her feel like she'd sold her body to Nathan. Alyssa clutched the sheets higher, glaring back.

"You're not even up yet," Piper accused him. "It's already eight thirty."

"Give me fifteen minutes." Nathan pulled on his discarded boxers under the covers and stood. "I promise. I'll be ready."

Piper cast another withering look at Alyssa and left the room. Nathan turned to Alyssa, and something told her this time she wouldn't be welcome.

"I'm going to go ahead. You don't have to come along this time. I'll see you later."

Despite being right and understanding his decision, his words hurt. Why would she go along? This relationship was a farce. Yet, it seemed like once he'd gotten between her legs, his desire for her to fully act the role of his girlfriend fizzled. Whatever. She could explore the island on her own, maybe even lie on the beach and enjoy the only vacation she might have in a long time.

"Of course. You go ahead. I'll keep myself occupied."

He cleaned up in the bathroom and was dressed within the time limit he'd given to his sister. "If you need anything, just ask Talia or Aziz. Felix will be with me."

She waved him off. "I won't need anything."

He hesitated with his hand on the doorknob and then turned back. "For last night, thanks."

Fingers curled in until her nails dug into her palms, she clenched her jaw and said nothing more. He really had to make it worse by thanking her for the damn sex. *Bastard!* Or was it the comfort food and letting him talk about his dad a little? Yeah, better to think of it that way. Then she could shake off the sense of being used. After all, he'd been concerned with her regretting giving in. She would *not* regret it, no matter what.

After Nathan left, Alyssa showered and dressed. In the dining room, she met Talia waiting for her. "Um…" The server table at the side of the room remained empty.

"I can make you anything you like, Ms. Alyssa. The cook has been given the morning off since it's unlikely anyone will be around the house. I'm a good cook. I've had training under her and my mother."

"Oh, no, thank you." Alyssa held up her hands. "I don't have much of an appetite either. I'm going to walk on the beach before it gets too hot and crowded."

The maid's brows went up. "The beach just beyond the house is private property. It will never be crowded."

*Damn, I forgot. The rich.* "Okay, thanks."

Alyssa left her shoes near the house and took the short trail to the beach on bare feet. Just as Talia mentioned, not a soul interrupted the landscape for at least a mile. Private homes dotted the shore, most as big as the Corde home. She started walking, taking her time and letting the chilly, clear water cover her feet before rolling back out to sea. Overhead, birds called to one another and dove into the water to catch fish. In the distance, even this time of morning, sailboats ambled along. She put her hand up and stared out at the peaceful scenery.

"Beautiful, isn't it?" came a deep voice behind her. She turned to spot a man standing close by with rolled-up jeans and a T-shirt that had seen better days. Not exactly dressed for the weather, but his dancing blue eyes gave her pause to admire the view onshore.

"It is." She hesitated. "You live around here?"

He chuckled, revealing even white teeth. "Me? No. I work there." He pointed in the general direction of one of the houses, smaller than Nathan's place. She guessed he worked as a servant. For some inane reason, she'd thought all the natives were black.

The man strolled closer and held out a hand. "Cullen James, and you?"

She shook her head at the hopeful expression on his face and hadn't missed how he checked out her ring finger. She put her other hand in his. Pretty bold for a servant. "Alyssa Jackson. Pleased to meet you. I'm just visiting."

"Ah, the upper crust. I'm sorry. I probably overstepped my bounds."

*Wow, bitter much?* She knew where he came from, though. "Actually I'm not rich. My...um...friend is. I'm bumming down here." Why the hell didn't she come right out and say her boyfriend? Probably because it felt wrong.

This man knew what it was like to struggle. She'd felt it in the roughness of his hands. The calluses didn't come from being born with a silver spoon in his mouth.

They fell into step side by side and continued along the beach. "Are you going to attend any of the beach parties?" he asked after some time.

She squinted against the rising sun. Damn, shades would have been a good idea. "That sounds like fun. I'm not sure."

"You should. I think you'd enjoy it. There's usually one at the beach outside the hotels, and maybe you'll let me buy you a drink. The music here is not to be missed."

She clapped her hands. "Oh, the steel drums! I'd forgotten about that. I want to hear them in real life."

His eyes brightened. "I'll take you to the best spot."

She stopped walking. Now was the time to tell him she wasn't available, which was a shame. He seemed nice, and he was sexy as hell. Aside from that, he was also a regular middle-class person like her. "Do you live here on the island?"

"No, we're down for the week. I was born and raised in New York."

Despite herself, excitement rose. "Me too!"

"So that's a yes to our date?"

Before she could answer, her cell phone rang, and she pulled it from her shorts pocket. Nathan's name flashed on the screen, and guilt assailed her. She glanced at Cullen. "I'm sorry, I have to take this. I can't go on that date. Probably wasn't meant to be, but it was nice meeting you."

She turned away and hurried down the beach in the direction she'd come while stabbing the connect button. "Hey, Nathan, everything okay?"

"Yes, everything's fine. I wanted to call and apologize for leaving you so abruptly this morning."

"Don't worry about it."

"Dad's fine. He just overdid it watching us play the game. Got too excited. They're letting him come home."

"That's great. So soon?"

He chuckled, and she heard the relief. "Trust me. He's better off at home, which is where he wants to be. The doctor believed he would wear himself down more wanting to be home and thinking he kept us from enjoying our time together. He also chewed my ass for not bringing you with me this morning."

"Me?"

"Yes, he's taken with you and said I was not treating you like family."

"Nathan, I don't feel right about deceiving him."

"He's happy, Alyssa. That is more important to me than a lie. Period. Are you backing out?"

She sighed and rubbed her damp forehead. "No, I'm not. It's just…"

"Good. I'll be home soon, and we can do something fun, just the two of us. Dad will need to stay in bed until tomorrow, so we're free."

"Fine. I guess I'll see you in a little while."

∽

"Are you serious?" Alyssa had trouble pulling in a breath

as she stared at the yacht anchored just feet away from where she stood. "We get to go on that?"

Seeing her excitement, Nathan grinned, and she thought he must be proud of himself. "Yes, it's mine. I figure I might as well get a little use out of it."

She croaked, "It's yours? Damn, it's huge. Does it have bedrooms in it?"

"Of course, but you'll never see them if you don't come on." He held out his hand, and she took it, her heart hammering out of control.

Yachts were synonymous with the wealthy as far as the average Jane was concerned, and she never imagined she'd get to go on one. As he escorted her around the vessel, she discovered Nathan's included four bedrooms, or cabins, as he called them. Eight people could sleep there, not including the space for the crew. The cute little kitchen with small eating area off of it impressed her, but he assured her the boat included a formal dining room as well.

"Do you throw parties here?"

"I have in the past. When Dad was well, he headed many corporate meetings here."

"That's the way to have a working lunch," she agreed.

He grinned.

"Well, for such a special treat, I can cook us lunch in the kitchen. That is if you have the refrigerator stocked."

"That's not necessary. I've hired a chef for the afternoon."

She shook her head. "Of course."

Soon they were under way, and rather than sit in the lounge, she opted for the deck and leaned on the rail at the front of the yacht. The breeze whipped her hair about, and the spray peppered her skin with drops of water. When she sensed Nathan watching at her side, she looked up at him.

"What?"

"You surprise me."

She raised a self-conscious hand to brush the damp hair from her face. "How so?"

"You're not worried about your hair or your clothes."

"Are you saying I look a mess?"

"Not at all. You're beautiful." He moved closer, but she took a step in retreat and turned away. When his hands dropped on her shoulders from behind, she couldn't bring herself to move out of reach. He nuzzled her neck. "Many of the women I've dated are concerned with appearances. They strip down to skimpy bikinis, but would not imagine getting into the ocean and damaging their hair with the salt water."

"Maybe you're dating the wrong women."

"I must be." The timbre of his voice gave her ideas she shouldn't have.

"How far are we going?"

"Far enough to be alone." He hesitated, and she glanced up at him. "Would you consider riding the jet ski? I can take you on mine, and you can hold me as tight as you need to."

Her eyes widened. "You only have one?"

He burst out laughing. There it was, that happiness she'd wanted to see. Was it really because of her?

"One each then," he promised. "Go get changed."

The day flew by, Alyssa loving every moment on the water with Nathan. Her hair sat in a tangled wet mess on her head, and her skin darkened even more than its normal cocoa brown to a rich chocolate. None of that mattered with the spray in her face and the wind exhilarating as she zoomed over the water's surface. Nathan stayed just ahead, but kept an eye on her.

"You're a natural," he shouted.

She threw an arm in the air and whooped. He laughed and circled around. Back and forth, they raced and then chased each other. When she grew tired, Nathan pointed, and she shaded her eyes to follow where he indicated. A small island lay directly ahead. The place looked deserted, but had a natural beauty in white sand, palm trees, and green foliage. Lighting the sky in hues of orange, the sun lay heavy on the horizon.

Nathan directed her to drive slowly toward the shore, but they turned off the motors when the water appeared about two feet deep. He hopped off and helped her. Tingles raced up and down her back at his touch, and Nathan drew her in close to kiss her lips. She luxuriated against his chest and shut her eyes.

"Hungry?" he murmured.

She nodded. "A little, but I can wait so we can explore a little."

A noise to her left caught her attention, and she realized one of his staff was collecting the jet skis. Nathan took her hand and led her up to the beach. "I've arranged for everything. You don't have to wait."

"What do you mean?"

Two more staff rowed a small boat to shore and began unloading picnic items, a table, chairs, a blanket, and even a basket with food and wine. Alyssa blinked at the elaborate setup. "Nothing's simple with you, is it?"

He shrugged. "You don't like it?"

"Don't be crazy." She approached the table, her stomach rumbling from all the exercise. A bite of pepper jack cheese calmed the beast a little. "Why did you do all this, though? Your family isn't here to see."

"My way of saying thank you—for yesterday."

"Oh."

She turned away, but he pulled her back. "Is that okay?"

"Sure, of course. Why wouldn't it be?" She dismissed the silly thoughts running through her head, and they sat down to eat. When Alyssa had had her fill, Nathan stood up and held out his hand.

"Let me straighten this a bit and throw out the trash." She started to pick up one of the plates, but a servant leaped forward to relieve her of it.

"Your job is to look beautiful," Nathan told her and led her over to the blanket. They stretched out in the evening sun.

Alyssa turned toward him and watched as Nathan put his hands above his head and shut his eyes. Even though he looked content, she sensed the tension. So much weighed on his shoulders. She might not command hundreds, maybe thousands, of employees, but she knew how he felt. She and stress were no strangers. His words echoed in her head, and she thought of Lydia.

"Do you think women shouldn't work?"

His eyes popped open. "Where did you get that?"

"I don't know. Just asking."

"Women can do whatever men can do."

She smirked. "The answer designed to keep a man out of the doghouse."

His wink made her wonder all the more, and he sat up to touch her cheek. "I am not a chauvinist, but I believe there's nothing wrong with a man taking care of a woman. If she chooses to stay home, and her significant other is okay with that, it's fine."

"Okay, I'll give you that one."

"Smart woman."

She stuck her tongue out at him. He made a grab for it, but she rolled away. He would not be put off. Before she knew what he planned, he landed on top of her while she faced downward, his cock pressed against her ass. Desire flamed to life, and the game ended as fast as it had started. Nibbling at her neck, he captured her wrists and pinned them to the blanket.

"I want to be inside you right now," he whispered in her ear.

She shivered. "Someone will see."

"No one is here but us."

"The servants, your crew…"

"I can order them to look away."

"Uh, yeah, no. Let me up, Nathan." She thought he would fight her or try convincing her again, but he did as she asked.

"Alyssa."

The serious tone made her look at him.

"Do you have someone back home?"

"If I did, I wouldn't be here, and I definitely wouldn't have had sex with you last night."

"I want you to be my mistress after this is all over."

Was he serious?

"As I said, it's a woman's choice as to the role she leads. I can already tell I want you longer than a week, and I can give you whatever your heart desires. I'm a generous man."

"All I have to do is keep pleasing you in bed."

"Correct."

He must have missed the bitter tone. No more nights wondering how she'd stretch the little she had over all the bills. No more ramen. At least, not until he grew bored with her.

"Don't think of it as one-sided, pleasure all for me and none for you. I believe you enjoyed the sex as well as I did."

"I'm not denying it." She struggled to contain her anger. He did nothing wrong asking, and yet, it felt like he was saying she wasn't good enough to be a full-fledged girlfriend, not a genuine one. Just a fuck buddy with the extra advantage of enjoying his money.

"I—"

"Excuse me, Mr. Corde, sir, but we need to get going. A storm is coming in."

At the crewman's words, Alyssa glanced toward the ocean and was surprised to see dark clouds on the horizon.

Nathan stood and pulled Alyssa to her feet. Their conversation was forgotten as they hurried to get things packed. Alyssa wouldn't hear of Nathan leaving it all to the servants. She did not want to be on the water when a storm hit. The thought alone sent chills of terror racing down her spine. By the time they made it back to the yacht, the rain had begun to fall, and the captain headed them back toward Grand Cayman.

The water grew choppy, and the yacht tossed about over the waves. Alyssa's stomach churned. She held on to the rail on deck until her fingers hurt. Nathan moved up behind her and laid his hands over hers. "Let go, baby. I need you to put on this life jacket."

She hesitated and then worked fast to get it on.

"You should go below. You're getting soaked."

"Hell no. If this thing goes down, I'm not going to be stuck below deck and drown."

"Alyssa."

"I'm not kidding, Nathan. I'm trying to keep it together."

Her teeth chattered, and her limbs shook. She prayed she wouldn't act like an idiot in front of him and his men, but it seemed like she already had. The crew nearby tossed her looks of concern that Nathan ignored. He kept his eyes on her.

"Everything will be fine." He wrapped his arms around her and drew her close. "I will make sure you're safe, and trust me, this yacht isn't going down easily. The storm is not as bad as it seems. It will be over quickly."

Lightning illuminated the sky, and thunder crackled, making her shriek in alarm. She sneezed one after another as rain soaked her hair, which had dried even in the early evening sun. When she began to shiver, Nathan pried her hands from the rail and picked her up.

"No, don't do that. We're unsteady."

He crushed her to his chest and strode with purpose to the door leading below deck. Alyssa buried her face against his neck. "If you drop me, I'm going to kill you."

A chuckle sounded above her head. Somehow he made it to one of the bedrooms without falling, or dropping her, and he sat down on the bed with her on his lap. His hold didn't lessen for an instant, and Alyssa clung to him, fighting panic. The boat continued to toss about, and the weird creaking from various corners drove her insane. Nathan's low voice and gentle words kept her from the edge.

"Everything will be okay. I've got you," he murmured, and she felt the vibrations in his chest. Concentrating on his heartbeat, she calmed down. A boat horn sounded, working her up again, and Nathan tightened his grip. "Shh, we're coming into port. See? It's fine."

She climbed off his lap and checked the window. He was right. Lights from the shore pierced the darkness. Her knees gave out, but Nathan was there behind her. He stayed close by while she changed into warm, dry clothes, and he did the same. Not soon enough, they were back on solid ground and headed to his house. Nathan laced his fingers with hers, sitting beside her.

"I hope the storm didn't ruin the day for you."

She thought of his offer and shook her head. "No, that didn't ruin it."

He appeared about to ask if she insinuated something else did, but thought better of it. Good. She didn't feel like talking about being his mistress. Not that she had any intention of saying yes. The answer would be no despite how much she enjoyed his touch. Nathan needed a woman impressed with his money enough to go after it any way she could. She was not the one. If he wanted arm candy, let him find it elsewhere. This week was the beginning and end for her, and then back to reality.

# Chapter Eight

No matter how many times Alyssa told Nathan nothing bothered her, he knew she lied. She'd felt distant most of the day and even turned away from his advances toward having sex the night before. He'd thought they had moved past the pretense that the attraction between them was feigned. They wanted each other. They had tasted and touched and explored. He desired more, and so did she. So why did she turn him down?

The fact that she grew restless but refused to explain her emotional state drove him crazy and heightened his anger. Was it the offer to become his mistress that upset her? She could say no. He would not like it, but he would accept her decision.

Frustration drove him to invite her to attend a party at a business associate's hotel. Maybe getting out of the house would help. Finding her by the pool, talking to his mother, he leaned over Alyssa and kissed her hair. He paused to breathe in her scent. Damn, she smelled good, like honey and brown sugar. Perhaps it was his imagination, or his cock, because he grew tight every time he neared her. His beauty's smooth cocoa skin drew his hands and beckoned to his lips to taste, but he gave in to no more than a stroke along her arm as he sat down.

"Excuse me, ladies," he said, "enjoying the day?"

"Of course, more with you here." Alyssa glanced up at him with such an expression of adoration he lost his train of thought. Then it occurred to him she was a pretty good actress.

His mother stood. "I'm going to let you lovebirds enjoy yourselves while I go check on Dad. He should be waking from his nap soon."

"Mom, you don't have to leave on my account," Nathan assured her.

"Nonsense. I was young once, and I've been monopolizing all of Alyssa's time today. I know she missed you when you were gone." His mother kissed them both and disappeared inside the house. He turned back to Alyssa, but she'd already risen and walked to the pool's edge to dip her toe in. The knot of frustration wound tighter around him.

"Would you like to attend a beach party with me tonight?"

She turned glowing eyes to him, and a smile transformed her already beautiful face. A wayward dark brown curl bounced between her eyes, and she brushed it away absently. He'd noticed her hair started out very black, but now the sun had browned it a bit. Something tightened in his chest watching her.

"Seriously? A beach party?"

Relief flooded him at her excitement. "Yes, I take it you want to go?"

"Ah, yeah!" She laughed. "When do you need me ready? I can wear one of the sundresses I bought, maybe the blue one."

He mentally went through all the clothing she'd shown him from her shopping experience and what she'd brought from New York. While he let his mind wander during the times his mother showed off her purchases, Alyssa had captured his interest, and he'd imagined her wearing each piece she had held up for him to see. Well, that and him peeling them off. "How about the green one with the low cut in the front?"

Her eyebrows rose. "That's so formal."

He nodded, stood up, and strode over to kiss her lips. *Careful, Nathan, or you'll have her in bed and not leave the house at all. Then how will you get that sweet smile again?* "How about seven thirty? Will that work?"

"Um, I guess so."

He examined her face and noted the doubt, but he knew she'd look amazing in the dress, and he would do all he could to help her to enjoy herself that night. Then later, maybe she would be willing to let him make love to her, and they could get back to where they stood at the beginning.

∽

Nathan kept his hand at Alyssa's lower back, guiding her through the entrance to the hotel. Just as he knew, Alyssa in her dress did things to shrink the room in his pants. He'd had to distract her to deal with his erection, but the more he took in the supple breasts and generous view at her dress's neckline, and the long, shapely legs peeking through a slit that extended almost to her hip, the less control he maintained over his body. Then he had led her out to the car and got a good look at that ass. All of his will kept him from tossing her over his shoulder and marching up to their room to rip her clothes off and have his way with her. Somehow, he needed to convince her to keep seeing him after the week ended. The very thought of any other man pushing into that tight, sexy body made him want to commit murder. She was his until he had sated the lust she invoked day and night.

"Mr. Corde," one of the hotel staff called out to him. Nathan sifted through his memory and the mental notes he'd made on every person he had ever met. The man's name popped to the forefront of his mind.

"John, how are you?"

The man's face glowed with pleasure. "Fine, thank you, sir. Mr. Cunningham's party is in the Waldorf Room. If you and your guest will follow me, I will show you the way."

As they walked, Alyssa glanced up at him. That sweet confusion made him squeeze gently at her waist.

"The Waldorf Room?" she whispered. "Isn't the party out on the beach?"

"There is a terrace outside the room," he informed her, "with a good view of the water."

"A view."

He peered at her, but she'd already turned to face the room they entered. Crystal chandeliers hung from various spots on the ceiling. Tables with pristine white tablecloths were arranged at one end of the room, dancing space at the other. No one took advantage of the latter. Most of the men, dressed in black suits, stood about talking to each other. Fewer women were in attendance, and those who were appeared to have chosen dresses that were the most vivid in color and showed the most skin. While some of them were quite beautiful, none approached Alyssa's perfection.

"Mark Cunningham." Nathan greeted the man he'd known for fifteen years but who was not exactly a friend. They'd been on the same side of the negotiating table a time or two, but more often the opposite. He had always felt Mark lived to one-up him, but then that might be his ego talking.

"Nathan Corde," the object of his thoughts bellowed and shook his hand. "Welcome to my hotel. She's impressive, isn't she? I've made quite a few renovations. I'll take you around later, and if you like, we can let our secretaries schedule us for time to talk about finding you one of these toys."

Nathan had trouble keeping the distaste off his face. "Thanks, but I have no interest in buying a hotel at this time."

Mark elbowed him. "Aw, don't be jealous, Nathan. You can't always be the winner, right? And who is this lovely lady, another mistress? I can't keep up with you."

Alyssa's lips tightened, and Nathan pulled her closer to his side. "This is Alyssa Jackson. Alyssa, Mark Cunningham, our host."

"Beautiful," Mark breathed and raised her hand to his lips. Nathan resisted smashing his nose and stuck his right hand into his pocket instead.

When he could without being rude, Nathan led Alyssa to meet other guests. Soon he fell into conversation about the stock market. He glanced in his lover's direction and found her several feet away, speaking with a couple of the women, and he relaxed a little more. She handled herself well, her head held high, a polite smile on her face. The two women she happened to converse with were not interested in much more than fashion and the net worth of their current lovers. He hoped Alyssa wouldn't be too bored.

A hand on his arm transferred his attention from Alyssa to the tiny blonde beauty at his side. "Nathan, I didn't know you would be here."

He stilled, wondering if it was worth removing his arm from her hold. "Hello, Natasha. I hadn't heard you were in the islands."

She pouted, pursing full pink lips. The white dress she wore clung to her figure like a second skin, and the neckline plunged so low, he expected any second to see nipple. Despite the blonde bimbo look, Natasha, heiress to a tidy fortune and former CEO of her father's oil company, had a brain in her head. The year before she had named a successor. Rumor had it she'd decided her next conquest would be him. He shouldn't have been surprised to see her.

"If you'd told me you were coming, I would have joined you."

He lowered his head toward hers so as not to be overheard and to make his point. "We had a brief affair. That's over. I don't see any reason to inform you of my activities."

"Aw, don't be like that, Nathan, baby. We were good together, and we can be again."

"Natasha," Mark boomed. "When did you arrive?"

Nathan gritted his teeth when Mark nabbed Alyssa and pulled her over to where he stood with Natasha. Alyssa's gaze had already been flitting between him and the blonde, lingering a fraction of a second on the spot where Natasha still wrapped around his arm.

"This is Nathan's date," Mark informed Natasha, and he knew what the man plotted. For years, he'd wanted Natasha, but she never gave him more than a nod. "I hear things are pretty hot and heavy between them."

Natasha's bow lips parted in her surprise. She didn't have to question out loud "a black woman" for him to guess what she thought. The disgust flashed over her features and was gone in a heartbeat. She held out long, slender fingers to Alyssa, the others still curled over his bicep. "Great to meet you. I'm Natasha Pyotr. Aren't you the daughter of that boxer—um, what's his name?"

"Natasha," Nathan growled.

"No, I'm not." Alyssa ignored the outstretched hand.

"Oh, I'm sorry. Goodness." Somehow Natasha managed to blush. "What do you do?"

Alyssa's chin rose. "I'm a business owner."

Several heads turned, and a couple people wandered over to them. Nathan disentangled himself from Natasha's hold and moved to Alyssa's side. While he rested a hand on her lower back, she straightened even more, causing his touch to fall away.

"What corporation?" Natasha insisted.

"I really don't think that's—" Nathan began.

"Jackson Books and Things." The pride in Alyssa's tone did not lessen the impact of her words upon the small crowd around them. Nathan saw the realization enter their eyes that she was most decidedly not from a well-to-do family, nor had she built up a fortune with her own skills and ability. He saw the dismissal in every face, except Mark's, who appeared gratified. Natasha maintained the false smile and friendly air that had won many to her side in business and in her personal life. He had grown to despise that trait in her, although he was not a stranger to manipulating people to get what he wanted.

"Oh, a little bookstore. That's so cute," Natasha cooed.

"Fuck you," was Alyssa's terse reply.

Several gasps rose among the crowd.

"E-Excuse me?" Color rose to an unflattering shade in Natasha's face.

Alyssa leaned closer to her and eyed her from head to foot. "I said—*fuck* you. I don't need you looking down on me. I don't care who you are."

"Alyssa." Nathan grasped her arm and whipped her around to weave through the crowd that had grown since they'd arrived. Where he could have easily scanned all the guests when they first walked through the door, now he had to force the way between bodies to get to the far end of the room. Leave it to Mark to invite more people than the room could hold with comfort, just to show off.

When they reached a door exiting to the hall, Nathan took it, shuffling a protesting Alyssa along with him. She yanked her arm free of his hold the moment they were alone and glared at him. He ran a hand through his hair and sighed.

"I apologize," he began. "I know the atmosphere in there was not what you're used to."

"The atmosphere?" She shook her head and put her hands on her hips. "It was more than the atmosphere. It was the skank who felt like she had to make herself look good by belittling me."

He extended a hand to her, but she moved away.

"Alyssa, you know your worth. Natasha didn't insult you."

Her eyes widened. "You're defending her?"

"I'm not." He felt the breach between them widening and searched for the right words. This was easier when it came to business. He didn't care to manipulate Alyssa. "I just feel—"

"That I was the rude one when I said fuck her."

"I didn't say that."

"I'm not stupid, Nathan. I know when a person smiles in my face and is cussing me out in their head. I'd prefer the honest type, but she's so not it. Look, I'm sorry I embarrassed you."

"You didn't."

"Liar."

"Alyssa…" He tried touching her again, but she moved out of reach.

"Don't even. This is your world, and you're welcome to it. I'm here for one purpose, and that's to be your girlfriend for your parents. They're not around, so have at it. Enjoy your friends."

When she started walking away, he shouted after her, "Where are you going?"

She didn't answer or look back. Instinct told him to follow and make her see reason, but anger kept him where he stood. She held him at a distance. He'd have to be a fool not to see it. Alyssa was not some ignorant woman who didn't know how to play the game. Her intelligence had shined through the way she expressed herself from the first day he met her. They could enjoy each other, so why the hell did she have to resist?

Turning to face the door leading into the party, he paused. The thought of dealing with Natasha in her bid for his attention, and every other man's in the room, didn't appeal. Yet, she'd been good in bed, *very* good, and she had an incredible body. An image of Alyssa's sexy figure slid into his mind, and he sighed. What to do?

# Chapter Nine

*hat kind of Jimmy John beach party was that?* Alyssa fumed. She stomped down the hall and made her way back toward the entrance of the hotel. When she turned a corner, she came to a spot where she could turn right or left. The right led to where she and Nathan had entered the building, but the left, she realized, led to the beach. Out there was what she'd expected, bare feet, and warm sand beneath her toes. She'd been shocked he wanted her to wear this fancy dress and high heels. Now she knew why. Bastard had no clue to fun.

An image of their time on the beach, sharing a picnic, came to mind, or riding the jet skis and swimming together, and she sighed. Okay, that had been fun, but it did not negate the fact that the man couldn't do without his servants. He probably never ate without silver utensils or licked rib juice from his fingers.

Still, a part of her had hoped he would follow and apologize, beg her to go to the beach with him for real. *Who am I kidding?*

She took a left and headed outside. The warm night breeze stirred a tendril of hair, and she started to feel a bit better. After slipping her shoes off, she started out along the path that quickly turned to sand. Her feet sank with each step closer to the water. Steel drums and laughter floated on the air, drawing her in that direction, and before long, she stumbled upon what she'd been looking for.

"Hey, come join the party," several men and women shouted in her direction. Someone raised a beer bottle in greeting. People gyrated to the music. A waiter happened by, and Alyssa ordered her own beer. Looking around, she realized she was way overdressed. Most of the partiers wore nothing more than shorts and T-shirts. Some of the women had forgone clothing completely and sported bikinis.

On impulse, Alyssa held up a finger to the waiter when he brought her drink. "Can you hold on to it just one moment?"

The man nodded, and she hurried away to the bathrooms not far off. She stripped out of her dress, glad she'd worn her own bikini in the mistaken thought that she and Nathan would get casual later in the evening. When she left the bathroom, she walked over to the outdoor bar. "Mind if I leave this back there?"

The bartender's interested gaze swept her figure, and he grinned. "Sure thing, miss. Have fun."

"Thanks. I will." She waved to him and ran back to the waiter holding her drink, tipped him, and swallowed a mouthful of beer. "Now that's more like it."

Glad her handbag was tiny and of soft material, she tucked it into the band of her bottoms and went to enjoy the music she'd been waiting to hear. She hadn't been there long before someone called out her name, and she turned, tensing, thinking to see Nathan.

Her eyes widened. "Cullen, what are you doing here?"

"Off work." He grinned. "Looks like you're enjoying yourself."

"I am now."

"Can I buy you a drink?"

She held up her beer. "Just starting, but"—she tilted her head to the side and surveyed him from head to foot—"you can dance with me."

They were soon swaying to the mellow tones, and Alyssa shook her hips and laughed at Cullen trying to dance. His gaze never left her face, and the attention went a long way to soothing her hurt feelings. Here, she didn't have to feel like she didn't measure up or that she'd say the wrong thing. Cullen treated her like she mattered even though there were plenty of beautiful women on the beach.

"Want to walk a little?" he offered, and she agreed. Under the moonlight and with the sound of the music fading, they strolled along the shore. Cullen reached for her hand, and she let him hold it. "You looked sad when I first saw you."

"Me?" She considered lying and bit her lip. "I guess I was a little. I went to one of those fancy parties and regretted it."

He stopped walking. "Let me guess, bunch of snooty people looking down their noses at you, talking about nothing but business?"

She laughed. "Oh no, we can't forget the two women that told me exactly how much my dress and shoes cost and where I bought them. Then they proceeded to advise me on where to go the next time."

His brows dropped low. "I'm sorry."

She waved her hand, shaking her head. "Don't worry about it. For those two, I really feel like they meant well. They had no clue how insulting they were. It was the other one."

"The other one?"

"I don't want to talk about her. How about you? How did your day go?" The truth was that Natasha bitch got under her skin more because of how she'd clung to Nathan and the way he didn't bother shaking her off. Right in Alyssa's face he had made it obvious they either had a thing going or had one previously. Even if she was a fake girlfriend, the least he could do was show her some respect. After all, he had invited her to the party.

"Alyssa, are you listening?"

She blinked. "Oh, yeah, sorry. What were you saying?"

He shared stories of dealing with the rich, having to take the blame for what he didn't do. Alyssa patted his arm and commiserated with his plight. He had her tearing up at the sad stories one minute and laughing at his jokes the next.

"I think you can be a writer," she told him.

His eyes widened. "Me? No. Don't tell me you don't believe me."

"Of course I do. I just meant the delivery is so good. You should make money off this stuff. Then again, I guess you'd lose your job if you exposed the crazy that's in your household."

To her surprise, he seemed to consider her words with all seriousness. "You, my beautiful Alyssa, have a good mind of your own. If I'm not careful, you'll make me fall in love. Then where will we be?"

She snorted. "Yeah right." She started to walk off, but he caught her hand and drew her back. A misstep landed her in his arms, and she sucked in a breath. "I think I should get back."

"Stay a while."

"I can't. It's late."

"Aren't you on vacation?"

She couldn't explain. Matter of fact, she didn't want to explain. Not if it meant he would stop talking to her. Being with him felt good, even if he didn't stir the longing that Nathan did. Cullen was fun in his own way, and the complication of wanting to spread her legs for him wasn't there to confuse her. *Okay, it might be nice to kiss him. No, that's wrong. I do not juggle two men at a time. Not my thing.*

"Tomorrow morning," he urged when she didn't say anything. "Meet me on the beach where we first met."

"I—"

"Alyssa!"

Her throat went dry, and she jerked from Cullen's hold. She peered over her shoulder and realized Nathan was storming in their direction. She couldn't see his face in the shadows, but she'd recognized the voice and with it the height and build. The moon behind the clouds made it likely he only guessed it was her standing there with no one else nearby.

She spun back to face Cullen.

"Don't say anything!"

"Don't say anything!"

She blinked at the fact that he'd spoken the same words, but then figured he meant pretend it wasn't her so she wouldn't have to leave. On her part, she wasn't ready to let this new friend go, so she didn't want Nathan and Cullen finding out about each other. She'd sunk low.

"Tomorrow," she assured him and darted along the sand until she reached Nathan. He grasped her arm and peered over her shoulder. She pushed past him and started walking in the opposite direction.

"Who was that?" he demanded.

"Just somebody I met at the beach party—the *real* one," she snapped.

"You alone in the dark with a man is not a party," he growled.

She stopped walking and put her hands on her hips, glaring up at him. "Excuse me? You're out here questioning my actions when that little blonde bunny wrapped herself around you so tight, she was practically in your boxers."

"You're exaggerating."

"Whatever." She started again, and he fell into step beside her until they bordered the partygoers, and light illuminated his face, a mask of anger. Now she knew he could get angry, but he still hadn't raised his voice. The controlled way he held himself in check would have been sexy if he hadn't pissed her off.

"So that's what this was, a childish way to get back at me? You picked up some strange man at a party where you know no one, and you walk off into the darkness with him half naked?"

When he put it like that, she did seem like an airhead, but she would not straighten him out with the truth. "Look, it's late. I'm tired. This night has been a joke, so if you don't mind, I want to go back to your house. If you won't take me, I'm sure I can find a ride somewhere."

She cast a glance in the direction of several men, and he grunted as if he would toss her over his shoulder at any second. Alyssa would cut him down to size if he even tried.

"I bet you could," he bit out.

"What's that supposed to mean?"

"Let's go. I will drive you."

"You mean your chauffeur."

"I don't understand the resentment you feel about my station in life, Alyssa. I swindled no one. I don't own sweatshops. I work damn hard for what I have, probably more than the average man."

"I'm not resentful. Just forget it. I'm going for another drink." She headed to the bar, but he followed.

"Where are your clothes?"

His words brought her dress and shoes to mind, and she leaned on the bar and called to the man behind it. "Hey, can I have my stuff now, please?"

He approached with an excited grin spreading over his face. His gaze lowered to her breasts, which were smashed a little on the counter. "I get off in half an hour. How about I give them to you then?"

Nathan crowded her from behind and dropped a threatening hand on the bar. "She'll have them now, and neither of us cares when you're off work."

The man paled. "Mr. Corde, of course, sir."

Alyssa groaned. "Does everyone know you and kiss your ass?"

Nathan's lips tightened into a straight line. "Not everyone."

"I know you're not talking about me, because if you are, you should get it by now. I'm never kissing your ass." She grabbed her dress and shoes and turned on her heel to stalk away. He caught up with her and directed her to the hotel. Now that she had left the beach, dressed the way she was, she couldn't wait to get out from under the bright lights.

They strode through to the front entrance where his car waited. Nathan didn't wait for his driver to open the door. He wrenched it wide, and she shuffled inside the dark interior. The snide remarks from her side and the cold parries from his continued on the road home.

"So what? I'm supposed to put up with any kind of treatment just because I'm pretending to be your girlfriend?"

"No one said you did, Alyssa. If you would just calm down…"

She managed to scramble into her dress, and she felt his eyes on her the entire time. Goodness knows she wasn't trying to entice the insufferable man when she wiggled to get the material to lie properly over her breasts. For some reason it felt tighter. "Calm down? It's not like you're paying me to do this, Nathan."

"Money, you bring that up a lot."

"You're counting. And no, it's not about money. It's about respect."

He growled in frustration. She rolled her eyes at him. When the car pulled to a stop, she jumped out and ran up to the front door. Aziz opened it before she got there, and she muttered her thanks before continuing up to the bedroom she shared with Nathan. He burned her up with that superior attitude. He didn't see where he was wrong, or his uppity friends. Well, he could kiss her ass. She would ask for another bedroom too, because it was for damn sure she wouldn't spend the night in the same bed with him.

Hearing him coming up the stairs, she slammed the door and headed toward the bathroom, chuckling under her breath. The move was childish, but at the moment, she didn't care. She turned on the hot spray and stripped her dress and bikini off. The bathroom door crashed against the wall, and she jumped, covering her breasts with one arm and cupping her pussy with the other hand.

"Get out, Nathan!"

His gaze full of rage swept her from head to foot, and if possible, it darkened. Her mouth went dry, and behind her arm, her nipples pebbled. To her annoyance, her pussy moistened just having him look at her.

"We were not finished with our discussion."

"Discussion? That's what you call it? Why don't you go have a discussion with Natasha? I'm sure she'd enjoy it. Me, I'm already bored silly."

He advanced into the spacious room. At her apartment, she would have been trapped. Here, she could run around like a mad idiot and maybe avoid him. Well, that would be if Nathan didn't have the speed and grace of a damn animal. She spun on her heel, about to jet, but he crossed the space between them and grabbed her arm. A sudden crouch to the floor surprised him enough for her to get free, but when she stood and took a step, he was on her once again. She stumbled and had to uncover her breasts to keep from slamming into the wall. Nathan had no mercy. He followed and pinned her there. *How the hell did I end up like this?* She drew in a deep breath and was glad he couldn't see her face at that moment. To be butt naked, pissed, and facing the wall and him so close behind was not a good thing.

"Why would I want Natasha," he demanded, "when I can have this?" His fingertips skimmed the back of her thigh up to her ass, and he squeezed. She shut her eyes and swallowed hard.

"I-I'm not going to be your mistress. What we did before…" Damn it, she couldn't say it. She couldn't flat out tell him no.

He released her arm and thumped the wall beside her head with a heavy hand. Even while he wanted her, the anger hadn't lessened. "You will not deny you want this, Alyssa."

She scowled over her shoulder at him. If she tried to move, her ass would brush his leg, or worse, she'd confirm he had a hard-on, and something told her there was no coming back from that knowledge. "If you're not going to get out, then move so I can take a shower. You're wasting water."

He stepped closer and bent his knees, bringing his pelvis in line with her ass. *No, no, no!* The barest touch had her back arching, and she stuck her butt out. Chin to her chest, she shut her eyes. The bastard played dirty.

He kissed her shoulder. "I want you." Another kiss landed at her nape. "You want me." He moved to the other side and nibbled her ear. "Nothing else matters."

She curled her fingers into her palms and sank toward the wall. He didn't follow, so she turned around to face him. Panting, she couldn't help her breasts rising and falling, and she had no energy to raise her hands to cover them. He stared as if mesmerized. Her stupid body responded to that alone. Looking at him made it worse, so she shut her eyes again, but she felt it when he neared. His lips touched hers. *Don't open your mouth, Alyssa.*

She parted her lips, and he snaked his tongue inside. Somehow, she broke the kiss. "We're not doing this."

"We're not?"

The rustle of clothing made her open her eyes. He undressed, and at the sight of his bare chest, she swore.

"Don't even think about it!"

His pants hit the floor, followed by his boxers.

"Why the hell!" She raged while taking in the angle of his cock, all hard and jutting from his body. The thought of sucking it flitted through her mind, on the heels of it pumping deep inside her pussy. Both ideas seemed impossible to walk away from. "This isn't fair. You need to give me space to make my own decision about whether to have sex with you, not seduce me into it. I thought it was important to you that I have no regrets."

The jumbled words seemed to have an effect. He backed off a step, and she sighed in relief.

"You're right. I apologize." All the anger appeared to drain out of him, and he turned his back.

Her gaze lowered to his muscled ass. Even that was pretty. Did the man have any physical imperfections? She lit on a small scar at the back of his right calf. No satisfaction came from knowing it existed. When he walked away, she followed his movements with hunger eating at her core. He opened the shower door and stepped through it.

"I will not follow him," she whispered to no one.

Even with steam rising, she saw through the glass door as Nathan raised his hands to his hair and let the water cascade over his form. He stood strong and erect, legs apart. His biceps flexed with his actions, and the gel he'd used bubbled on his taut skin, glided down his abs, and coated his muscular thighs. He turned around, facing her way, his eyes shut, and she was drawn not just to his body but him, the enigmatic man. She wanted to be near him, to hear him speak, to have him look at her and listen to her.

"You're an idiot, Alyssa." She stumbled toward him as if there were an invisible cord drawing her closer. He seemed to sense her and opened his eyes. For a moment, they stared at each other, and then he opened the door and stood aside. She joined him. He made no effort to touch her but waited for her to make the first move. "I'm not going to be your mistress."

"Okay."

She squeezed around him to get closer to the water and let its warmth ease some of her tension. After working gel into suds in her sponge, she began smoothing it over her body. Still Nathan didn't touch her.

"This thing we're doing." She licked her lips. "It's just this week. You can do what you want to do. We aren't exclusive."

What the hell was she thinking? She'd just broken it off with a guy because he wanted her and any woman who crossed his path, too. No, this wasn't the same. Nathan wasn't her boyfriend, and if she kept it straight in her head, she might never let her feelings for him grow to love. If he could sleep with whomever and she knew it, she could walk away with her heart intact. After all, they were from two different worlds, and she'd never thought she had the kind of hang-ups she'd displayed in the last few days. That also made it easier. *Good, it's settled.*

She held out the sponge to him. "Can you get my back?"

He took it and began stroking the ball over her skin. Tingles skidded along her spine despite the fact that he hadn't touched her with his hands.

"Are you sure about this, Alyssa?" He sounded doubtful.

"Why not? Men…and women…do it all the time. No big deal. Like I said, we aren't in a relationship, and this arrangement isn't permanent. We're having a little fun. Nothing wrong with it."

"You said before you didn't want an open relationship."

Damn, had she said that? "Oh, well, we're not together."

Nathan dropped the sponge and spun her to face him. He drew her close and wrapped his fingers at her waist to raise her in his arms. Together they stood beneath the stream, and when he kissed her lips, she forgot all protests, everything except him and the way he felt, the way he smelled, and his taste. She breathed him in, her lids heavy from the drunkenness that he caused. Her heart threatened to beat out of her chest, and her breaths—when he let her drag in air—were noisy.

"Right now, there's just you and me." He kissed her again and turned off the water while still holding her. She protested when he stepped out of the shower and didn't let her go.

"Nathan, put me down. We have to dry off."

His hold loosened, and she slid down a few inches. The head of his cock pushed against her pussy entrance. She moaned.

"If you make that noise, how will I let you go?"

"How am I going to keep quiet when your dick is about to slide into me?"

He shrugged. They stood there in the middle of the floor, him taking all of her weight without a problem. She held on to his shoulders, dripping wet and trying not to give in, but her heat was moist and ready. One more inch and he'd fill her.

"Nathan," she begged.

He allowed her to fall a little more, and she cried out his name once again. His cock pierced her sex an inch. She had to have more and wriggled her hips. A hiss escaped between his teeth. When she raised her head, she caught the same hunger she felt glimmering in his eyes, but his grip tightened.

"Not yet."

She let her head fall back and shut her eyes. "You want to torment us both."

"Isn't it good?"

"Yes." She panted, trying to get it together. The effort cost too much energy. Nathan lowered her down his shaft until he filled her to capacity, and then he raised her higher. She clenched his shoulders. "More."

"You want all of it, baby?"

A tremor shook her, and she nuzzled his neck, snaked her tongue along his throat, and sucked with gentle pressure at his Adam's apple. This time, he moaned, and she grinned in satisfaction.

He brought her down again and then back up. Her pussy walls seemed to swell around his dick, squeezing it. She exercised her internal muscles, trying to keep him where she wanted him. Nathan palmed her ass to maintain control. He set the pace, and no matter how much she pleaded, he didn't speed up or slow down. Her body thrummed to the beat he set, and nothing she did changed the fact. She kissed his lips, along his strong neck, and even tweaked his nipples. The man gave in to moans of pleasure but nothing more.

"Nathan."

"Yes, baby," he murmured, "say my name. Tell me how I make you feel."

"You're a bastard," she complained and struggled against the wonderful onslaught of his cock grinding into her, only to be taken away. Her core wound tighter, escalating toward an orgasm, but every time her thighs began to quiver, he stopped moving. "You're driving me crazy!"

"That's the aim, sweetheart."

She looked into his eyes, frowning. "Is this payback for what I said?"

"You think I would punish you by not letting you come?"

"I don't know."

She tried reading his expression, but couldn't determine what he thought or if he was still mad. Was this on purpose? Did he intend for them both to find satisfaction?

She opened her mouth to demand to know the answer, but he brought her down hard on his cock, and she screamed in delight. He turned and strode toward the closed door, but rather than open it, he thumped her against it, withdrew his cock, and thundered home in her pussy again.

"Yes, yes!"

Now her hands shook, and her thigh muscles spasmed so much, she teetered on the edge of an orgasm. Unable to hold on to him, she depended on his strength, but he had no problem pinning her to the door and thrusting into her over and over.

"How can I deny myself this, let alone you?" His words were slurred, lust filled, and heavy. "You have no idea how tight your pussy is and how little I can resist being inside it. Do you feel the way you squeeze me?"

"You're so big," she whimpered.

"No, you make me swell."

"Nathan."

"Damn it, woman, what you do to me." He pounded her harder, and his pelvis rubbed her clit each time, driving her desires higher. In the morning, she would be sore, but right now...*let it never end...*

Nathan hung one of her legs over his forearm. The other he shifted farther until her ankle rested on his shoulder. Her ass rose and spread, and still he ground deep into her wetness. The moist sounds their bodies made as they came together, along with the slap of their flesh meeting, took her plummeting over the precipice. She shouted his name one last time, and then she couldn't hold back even if she tried. Her orgasm took hold, and she sobbed in pleasure. Nathan didn't stop pumping into her until he, too, found his release, and then his pace eased, slowing to stillness.

He let her stand, but her knees gave, and he zipped her into his arms again.

"It's okay. I can—"

"Shh."

He nodded toward the doorknob, and she opened it for him to carry her through to the bedroom. By now, with all their lovemaking, they were dry, so she didn't protest when he laid her on the bed. Longing to be in his arms consumed her, but he didn't deny either of them the pleasure. He sank down beside her and stroked her hair from her face.

"You're beautiful. Do you know that?"

She suppressed a smile. "Who me?"

"Silly woman."

He didn't need to see how his words affected her, so she lowered her head and nestled against his neck. She shivered when he ran a thumb over her anus.

"I want to take you here. Is that okay?"

"What?"

"If you're afraid, I won't. Don't worry about it."

She looked at him. "I'm not afraid." She'd had it before and liked it with the right man who knew what he was doing. Did Nathan? Usually, she didn't go so far with a lover unless they were in a committed relationship. Despite the temporary status of her and Nathan, she wanted to do it with him. *Which is probably why I shouldn't.* "Oh crap, we didn't use a condom."

Her words couldn't have been more of a splash of cold water on him. He sat up. "Is there danger of you getting pregnant?"

"No."

He studied her face, and she could just guess what thoughts roamed his mind. She had no reason to try to trap him, and it was his ass that teased her in the bathroom and wouldn't let her go. He'd first seduced her, not the other way around. She saw when he came to that conclusion.

"I apologize." He rose from the bed. Something told her the sex wouldn't continue tonight. *Damn.*

She rose and found a clean nightie from the drawer and drew it on. Then she clicked off her bedside lamp and climbed into bed. Nathan moved around in the bathroom a while, but she ignored him. Eventually, he came to bed, and she pretended to be asleep.

"Alyssa."

"What?" She tried to keep emotion out of her tone, but failed.

"Turn around. I want to hold you."

Something warmed inside her. She resisted a little longer and then rolled over. He drew her close to his bare chest, and she luxuriated in the feel of him. They were just a bit too intimate for her liking, but she melted into his hold anyway. He encircled her in his arms and stroked her hair. When he pushed a leg between hers, she let him, and they snuggled tight from chest to thighs. After some time, she began to drift off, forgetting everything except Nathan.

# Chapter Ten

Alyssa came downstairs the next morning well rested if a tad sore between her legs. Just outside the dining room, she caught the sound of angry voices and paused. Maybe the family needed some time to sort out whatever their issues were. Nathan had left their bed early with a note to her that he had something to take care of. He would meet up with her in the afternoon. For some reason, she thought of Natasha, but pushed the woman from her mind. The more likely explanation was probably work. The man never rested. She'd like to see the day he had no responsibilities whatsoever.

Something Piper said pulled Alyssa from her thoughts. "I can't go because I've...got a prior engagement."

"What prior engagement?" Lydia demanded, and Alyssa thought the woman sounded like her son. She had never imagined Lydia angry, but now that she was, her tone matched Nathan's. That surprised her because she would have thought he got the controlled and calculated trait from his dad. "Explain to me why we agreed to spend time with Dad this week, and even when you're here, you act like you want to be somewhere else. Now you're saying the rare time Dad is strong enough for an outing, you're busy. Even Nathan says he'll be back in time. So who is this person you're seeing?"

"It's someone important to me."

A shiver raced down Alyssa's back. If she didn't miss her guess, Piper was ready to come clean, and she would not be around to witness the possible fallout. The Cordes were friendly, and in the face of Nathan bringing home a black woman as the love of his life, Leo Corde had not batted an eye. What would he feel about his daughter being gay? No one could predict that. Either way, she would not be around to find out.

Forgoing breakfast, Alyssa darted down the hall and took a side door outside. She removed her sandals and started around the path to the back of the house and down to the beach. Only when the long stretch of shoreline came into view did she remember Cullen's invitation to come where they'd first met. Damn, she was not feeling him today, or any man for that matter. Nathan's actions and attitude the night before confused her, so she wanted time to think on her own.

She turned in the opposite direction than the one she'd taken that morning of meeting Cullen, but she hadn't taken three steps before she heard him calling her name. Didn't the man have work to do? Or was he the type to slip out and do his own thing when no one was looking?

"Alyssa, wait," he called and jogged over to her. Even his movements were fluid and graceful, his sculpted calves golden brown from the sun. He looked as good as the last time, dressed in white shorts and a white T-shirt.

"Don't you ever work?" She smiled. "How's it going?"

He grinned. "Not when the boss is away on business."

So she had been partially right. "Don't I know how that is. Even on vacation, they are not."

"Can I take you to lunch? Better yet, I have use of my boss's boat. We could make a day of it."

Her eyes widened. "Won't he find out? I don't want you to lose your job."

He held up his hands as if that explained it. "I'm a jack-of-all-trades. I drive the car, sometimes the boat. If minor repairs are needed..."

Oh, he was the chauffeur, not a servant in the house. If his employer had left the islands, of course there wouldn't be work. She sighed. "Listen, I appreciate your offer and your interest in me. If this was another time and place..." She bit her lip. "Maybe we can catch up when we're in New York, but right now, I'm with someone. He's..." She thought of Nathan. What could she say? Not the truth. If Cullen's boss ran in the same circles with Nathan, and Cullen told him of her fake status, it could get around, and the Cordes did not deserve that. Not with all they dealt with in Leo's health already. "He's important to me."

Cullen's gaze flashed anger, but then it was gone. He smiled and took her hand. "I understand. Damn my timing, huh? I hope you'll give me a chance to be your

119

friend. I feel like we get each other. If not, I'll just have to hope to see you in New York. Can I give you my number?"

She hesitated and then nodded. After all, things with Nathan were coming to a close. That could not be avoided. She wouldn't be his mistress, and he hadn't offered anything else.

Cullen stroked her cheek. "I hope he recognizes what he has."

She lowered her gaze to the sand. "Thanks. I have to go."

By the time she reentered the house, all lay in silence. The dining room had been cleared out, but the moment she crossed the threshold of the room, Talia appeared. Alyssa started. "Oh, Talia. Is it okay if I make myself a sandwich in the kitchen? I know I'm late for breakfast."

"No, ma'am. You can't serve yourself."

Alyssa rolled her eyes. "I think I can, and I will."

The maid followed her through to the kitchen and hovered while Alyssa searched the refrigerator. The cook stared but said nothing. Alyssa had the feeling they both thought her insane.

"There you are, Alyssa."

She turned at Leo's voice and found him leaning hard on a cane. "Are you okay, Leo?"

The older man glanced around the expansive kitchen. "I don't think I've been in here. Odd. Talia, two sandwiches, please. One for me and one for Alyssa. Join me in the dining room, won't you, my dear?"

She couldn't ignore him and sighed. While he had relayed the message to Talia, the cook was the one who started on the food. Alyssa gave in to defeat and followed Leo. They took seats at the table, and soon Talia brought iced tea for her and coffee for Leo. He waited to speak until she left. Breakfast hadn't been that long ago, but apparently Leo wasn't in the dining room when Lydia and Piper argued. Of course they wouldn't have done it with him around and risk overtasking the man.

"How is my son treating you? Has he spoken of a ring yet?"

Alyssa froze in the act of sipping her tea. "Um, not yet." Damn, she couldn't continue to lie to him, not in his face and with him looking so feeble. Their sandwiches arrived, and she busied herself taking a bite of hers while her appetite evaporated.

Leo winked and patted her hand. "You have nothing to worry about. I think he will soon if I know my son."

*You don't know him at all, it seems.*

"I'm not holding my breath." She could have bitten her tongue at how harsh she sounded and scoured her mind for words to mend the situation.

"Sounds like you two have had a spat?"

She cursed Nathan for putting her in this situation. "Not exactly." Then she tried for the truth. "Sometimes he pisses me off. I mean, last night he said we were going to a beach party, and we get there, and it's some stuffy hotel shindig. A blonde bimbo insulted me, and that fool took her side. Crap, I must sound like an immature brat."

"You sound like a woman who demands to be treated with respect. There's nothing wrong with that. I prided myself on raising my kids to respect others no matter their station in life. Everyone has value. Perhaps I need to have a talk with the boy."

Alyssa shifted in her seat, wanting to escape. Leo did not need to get involved. "I'm good. Thanks. I can handle him."

The man's eyes sparkled despite the tired appearance around them. "I knew you were the right one as soon as I saw you."

She could find nothing to reply to this.

Leo leaned toward her and lowered his voice. "Let me let you in on a little secret about dealing with Nathan."

"Um, okay."

"Whatever he says or does, give him the benefit of the doubt if it upsets you. He is a good man, and often there's more to why he does what he does than you know."

So what did she do with that little tidbit? Leo hadn't really given her much to work with in understanding Nathan. Even if he did, she was not a doormat. Leo might or might not know his son, but he didn't know her.

"I'll keep it in mind," she said rather than question him further.

Lydia appeared in the doorway. "There you two are. I wanted to let you both know we're having guests for dinner tonight." The way she almost bounced into the room spoke volumes, but Alyssa decided not to speculate on why. Maybe Lydia got off on having people over. Of course, some did. She almost never had visitors, but that wasn't by choice. If her neighborhood were better, she would entertain. As it was, she had a hard time convincing Trinity to visit. Instead, they spent time together at her cousin's or at her uncle's house.

Lydia's popping about giving instructions to Talia, Aziz, and the cook somehow prevented her from getting around to sharing who was coming to dinner. Extra maids were called in to give the house a good scrubbing, although Alyssa hadn't spotted even a speck of dust in the place. She managed to stay out from underfoot of all the activity. She swam in the pool, walked the beach, and took an afternoon nap. The idleness after the long hours running her bookstore felt incredible. She might as well soak it up.

The white dress she chose for the evening featured ruching at the center front, highlighted with a rhinestone-and-beaded brooch. The halter V neckline extended over her shoulders to crisscross in the back. She loved the soft material and how the dress ended just above her knees—not too short or too long, a simple style yet elegant at the same time. When Nathan strode into the room, she was just slipping into medium-heeled silver slingbacks. He paused upon spotting her, and she waited for the verdict.

"Incredible."

Pleasure warmed her from head to foot, and she lowered her gaze to hide it from him. "Thanks."

He strode over and rested his hands at her waist. When he leaned in to breathe deep at her neck, she bit her lip at her body's reaction.

"You smell good enough to eat. Forget dinner and stay here with me."

"Lydia won't hear of that."

He sighed. "You're right. Do you know who's coming to dinner?"

Her eyes widened. "You don't?"

He shrugged. "Mom is too excited to sit still more than a second. I tried asking Dad, and he doesn't know either.

Then again, he always did indulge her. As long as she's happy, he's okay with it."

She studied his face, wondering if he would be that way with the woman he fell in love with. Not her concern. She shook her head and moved out of his hold. He loosened his tie and pulled his rumpled shirt from his pants.

"I'll be ready soon. Work took longer than I thought it would."

"Does it follow you around the globe?"

"Alyssa."

She shrugged. "Whatever." Before he could grab for her again, she moved away. A bit of last-minute rearranging of her hair, since a few pins had escaped the style she'd put it in, and she was all set. "I'm going down."

"Wait for me." He strode into the bathroom naked, and she took in the sight of his back, ass, and thighs with a sigh.

"Is that an order?"

He peeked out from the bathroom. "Please."

She rolled her eyes at him. "Fine."

To the sound of his chuckling, she moved to the window and pushed the curtains aside. A dark car was just pulling up the drive. She strained to see as they disappeared from sight, and curiosity sent her to the doors leading out to the balcony. Voices rose from the driveway, Lydia's unmistakable manic tones included. Alyssa leaned out to get a better look. A knot formed in her belly, and her fingers spasmed on the rail.

"Get a look?"

She jumped and turned around. Nathan stood in the doorway.

"Sweetheart, what's wrong?"

Did she dare tell him the truth? Better to do it now rather than deal with the drama later. Why the hell would Cullen be a dinner guest, and the woman with him was without a doubt Piper's girlfriend. Had she told her mother the truth about them and Lydia had been that excited to invite her over? That seemed unlikely.

Then she remembered. Of course, Cullen had mentioned being a chauffeur. Stupid. And he'd been dressed up because many of the rich families required their servants to wear a uniform. Why had he gotten out of the car and gone inside, though? Maybe he knew Aziz or Nathan's chauffeur and wanted to shoot the breeze with them until time to drive his employer home. Of all the dumb luck, though, that he'd work for her.

"Alyssa?" Nathan stood above her. She hadn't seen him move.

"I didn't see. They were inside before I got out here." That bought her a little more time to think this through. She'd told Cullen they couldn't see each other, and she'd done nothing wrong. Not exactly. Yet, knowing it didn't stop the guilt and nerves fighting each other in her belly.

When Nathan was dressed, they descended the stairs to the first floor together. He held her hand and drew her to his side when they reached the bottom. Voices from the living room led them in that direction, and Alyssa drew in a deep breath. Her balance off, Nathan had to tighten his hold a couple times, and she felt his gaze on her but refused to look up at him.

"Are you okay?" he whispered. "You're not getting sick?"

"No, I'm fine." Her heart hammered until she wondered if he heard it.

They entered the living room to find everyone present, including Cullen. The man's blue gaze snapped to hers, but not a lick of recognition shone in their depths. The friendly smile did not waver.

"Oh, here is Nathan and his sweetheart now," Lydia chirped.

The woman at Cullen's side was indeed Piper's lover, but as much as she smiled, Alyssa sensed her anger. Why should she be angry when they were finally admitting to the relationship? From Lydia's open happiness and Leo's calm acceptance, the two women should be relieved.

"Cullen, of course you know Nathan, but this is Alyssa," Lydia went on. "Alyssa, this is Cullen, Piper's boyfriend she's been keeping a secret from the entire family."

"No way," Alyssa blurted.

"Hell no," Nathan growled.

All conversation stopped, and the fake smiles from the younger people died away. Nathan glared at Cullen as if he was two seconds off rearranging his face. Piper clenched her hands at her sides, scowling back at her brother. The girlfriend—what was her name?—seemed just a bit in love with Nathan at that moment. Alyssa tried processing what she'd just heard around her own rising anger.

"You know each other?" she repeated.

"Of course." This time Leo spoke from his seat near the window. "The James's and the Cordes have known each other for years. Their vacation home is not far from here, and they have holdings out of New York."

"Smaller holdings," Nathan found need to add.

Cullen's jaw twitched. She figured Nathan had made the dig on purpose. So there had to be history between them. Well, the lying bastard deserved that and more, making her think they were on the same level, trying to make it in the world.

Lydia came over and swatted Nathan's arm. "Now, don't you start, Nathan. I know you two had a little tiff years ago, but it's all water under the bridge. I just wish your parents were in town, Cullen, so they could have come over. Oh, where are my manners? This young lady is Cullen's sister, Emma. Everyone sit down. Let's have drinks. Talia?"

They took their seats, Nathan all but pulling Alyssa onto his lap. He wound an arm around her shoulders and sealed her to his side. She shifted in her seat to get more comfortable, noting how Emma was just about to take the love seat with Piper but instead took an armchair. Cullen parked his stocky frame next to Piper, and neither seemed happy about it.

Alyssa welcomed the cosmopolitan she'd requested and took a huge drink to settle her nerves. Nathan claimed her free hand, lacing his fingers between hers. She frowned up at him. What was with the overaffection all of a sudden? Did Cullen threaten him with his presence? She needed to set the man straight. Cullen no longer interested her in the least.

"How long have you two been seeing each other?" Leo asked Cullen and Piper. His daughter paled and remained mute. Cullen opened his mouth to answer, but Nathan released Alyssa and leaned forward.

"Doesn't matter. It's not going to continue long."

"I think I can decide who I date, Nathan," Piper snapped.

"Really?" Ellen chimed in.

Alyssa grabbed Nathan's arm and whispered in his ear, "Do you think now is the time to voice your disapproval of the relationship?" She flicked her gaze in Leo's direction, and the fight left her lover in a heartbeat.

"You're right. I apologize, Dad, Mom, for my rudeness."

Alyssa rolled her eyes. He didn't feel the need to excuse himself to Cullen or his sister. Piper's red cheeks said she didn't appreciate the slight, and Alyssa saw a flash of something in Cullen's eyes. She was so over this dinner already, and they hadn't yet sat down to eat.

"Dinner is served, Mrs. Corde," Talia announced.

Lydia stood up. "Let's go in, everybody."

Aziz assisted Leo, and when Alyssa stood, she found Cullen at her elbow. His smile transformed his handsome face. "Can I take you in?"

Nathan slapped him on the back too hard and smiled, leaning in close to the man. "How can you do that without arms?"

Alyssa bit off a curse. "I think I can get into the dining room under my own steam."

She walked ahead of them, ignoring the muttered oaths from both men behind her. At the dinner table, Nathan held her chair and sat between her and his father, who headed the table. Lydia occupied the end opposite her husband, and Piper sat on her right. Rather than Cullen taking the seat next to Piper, he swiped the open spot on Alyssa's right, and Emma sat next to Piper. Nathan's glare should have struck the man dead.

"Hey."

Nathan glanced down at her when she caught his sleeve. She reached up to stroke his cheek and pressed her lips close to his ear.

"The jealousy thing is getting old. Can you tone it down? I think everybody gets it. I'm yours. It's starting to be obvious that it's fake."

He blinked at her, and if she didn't know better, she'd get the impression he thought her thickheaded. The insult rankled, and she scowled at him. Sensing Cullen had shifted closer to her, she turned in his direction. When his father engaged Nathan in conversation, Alyssa took the opportunity to question Cullen.

"I thought you were a chauffeur."

His eyes widened. "I never said that."

"You never said you were rich."

"I'm not on the Cordes' level. Believe me."

She didn't even bother to dignify that comment with a response, and he turned on the charm, covering her hand in her lap and stroking the skin. She tugged to get free, but he refused to let go.

"You're a lying bastard. Let me go."

His face almost met hers. The man was too obvious. "I only wanted you to give me a chance, Alyssa. When I first saw you get out of the car the day you arrived—"

"Wait, you knew I was here?"

"I only saw a beautiful woman I wanted to get to know."

She thought back trying to remember if she and Nathan had shown each other affection to indicate they were a

129

couple. Cullen might have thought her Nathan's secretary, down to help him with work, or even a new servant. Because of who he was, he might have been hesitant in case he intimidated her.

"Forgive me," he pleaded. "I never meant to hurt you."

"Please, I'm hardly hurt. We don't know each other like that."

"Then say I'm forgiven. I promise I just wanted to get to know you better, and there wasn't time to explain everything before my sister asked me to pose as Piper's boyfriend."

Alyssa peeked at the others around the table. No one appeared to pay them any mind at the moment. She lowered her voice a little more. "You know she's gay?"

He nodded, his expression matter-of-fact.

"Can anyone get in on this conversation, or should we give you two time alone?" Piper snapped from across the table. Emma bumped her shoulder, but Piper glared at Alyssa.

*Like I want to steal your fake-ass man.*

She managed to retrieve her hand from Cullen's grasp and twisted in her seat to meet Nathan's furious stare. "How do you know him?"

She opened and closed her mouth a few times. Had he seen Cullen touch her? No, he couldn't have. Something told her Nathan would have put Cullen on the floor, but that would take his act too far. "He was the guy on the beach."

Nathan set his cloth napkin on the table, and she grabbed his arm.

"Nothing happened." Why was she defending herself? He had no right to question her. Well, not entirely. Then she got it. This wasn't about her. Cullen had arrived pretending to be Piper's boyfriend, yet he kept hitting on Alyssa. Nathan wouldn't stand for that kind of treatment of his sister.

The tedious dinner stretched on with Alyssa focused on Nathan, leaning into him and hanging on his every word, the devoted girlfriend. He reciprocated the affection, but a sixth sense told her his anger hadn't cooled, perhaps directed at her and at Cullen. After a dessert of double chocolate cake and vanilla ice cream, which she refused, the family and their guests returned to the living room.

"Dad, are you okay?" Piper said, and Alyssa tightened the hand she'd laid on Nathan's arm. The muscles beneath it tensed. She glanced over at Leo, who appeared paler than earlier.

The older man forced a smile. "I'm just happy my little girl has found someone. Maybe there are grandchildren in our future, Lydia, from both our son and daughter."

Lydia clapped her hands together. "Yes, isn't it wonderful?"

Cullen slid to the edge of his seat. "Hold on, I—"

"It's been a good day for us, darling." Lydia stood and strolled to Leo's side. "I think we should leave the rest of the evening to the young people."

"You're right!"

Alyssa didn't like how he seemed hopeful they would all get up to making those grandchildren the second they were alone. As soon as the door closed behind his parents,

Nathan sat back in his seat and took Alyssa's hand in his. He laced his fingers with hers, but he didn't look at her. All of his attention lay on Piper. His sister fidgeted in her chair, Emma stared out the window, eyes glazed, and Cullen snuggled close to Piper's side in a belated attempt to appear the besotted idiot.

"So," Nathan began, the word somehow a warning no one could mistake, "why are you pretending to be my sister's boyfriend?"

Gasps sounded all around the room, including Alyssa's. She couldn't believe Nathan had called Cullen out for a liar. If nothing else, she thought he would believe the man a no-good cheating bastard who couldn't keep his attention on the woman at his side.

"E-Excuse me?" Cullen stuttered.

Why had she been attracted to him?

"I said"—Nathan's gaze shifted to Cullen, shutting the man up with a glance, and then back to Piper—"why have you lied to Mom and Dad, Piper?"

Talk about calling the kettle black. "Nathan," Alyssa chided, "leave her alone."

They waited for Piper to speak, but instead she jumped to her feet and ran out of the room.

"Piper!" Emma started after her, but Alyssa cut her off.

"I'll go talk to her." *What's gotten into me?* Emma stepped back.

Alyssa found Piper at the end of the hall, but instead of tears, as she expected, her lips were compressed into a straight line, and her eyes almost crackled with fire. *I don't need this drama.* "Piper, are you okay?"

"Get my brother to back off."

"Whoa." Alyssa held up her hands. "Look, I have nothing to do with this. It's between you and your family. What I want to know is why, when you were so close to coming clean with your mother, you didn't do it."

Confusion colored the woman's face and then cleared. "You overheard us talking this morning."

"Couldn't help it. I was on the way to breakfast."

"I wondered why…Never mind. Just talk to Nathan. If he doesn't stop acting like he's going to rip Cullen apart, we can't keep the act up."

Alyssa tapped her foot. "I don't know why you think you can command me and I'm supposed to jump."

Piper gritted her teeth. "*Please*."

"Of all people to bring here." She tried again to reason with the woman. "Why don't you tell them the truth? You're an adult, aren't you? I think Nathan said you're twenty-four."

Piper snorted. "I'll never be an adult in my parents' eyes."

"No, you'll never be an adult until you start acting like one."

"You wouldn't understand."

For some reason that hurt, given she had no parents, but she didn't think Piper meant it that way. "No, I don't, and I don't give a damn either. Handle your business."

She turned on her heel and marched away. Piper didn't try to stop her and didn't return to the living room. After some time, Emma jumped up from her seat and left without a word. Alyssa sighed.

Nathan rose and approached the wet bar. He poured himself a drink and looked toward Alyssa. She shook her head. He didn't attempt to serve Cullen. When neither Piper nor Emma returned, Cullen stood. "Perhaps it's best I leave for now."

Nathan downed his drink. "Better yet. Don't come near my family again."

Cullen scowled, started to say something, and thought better of it. He faced Alyssa instead. "Alyssa, it was great seeing you again. Please, when you're back in New York, look me up."

"She won't."

"Nathan, enough!" She moved ahead of him to escort Cullen to the door. Aziz appeared from nowhere to open it, and all of them froze. Rain poured in great sheets, and the sky hung heavy with dark clouds. Even before Aziz could respond, a gale wind swept in and almost whipped Alyssa off her feet. Nathan's arm came around her waist, and he hauled her back to his chest. Not for the first time, she appreciated his strength.

"You may stay until this is over," he said with grudging acceptance. Alyssa suspected if Cullen had been alone, Nathan would have kicked him out into the storm. He didn't have such strong feelings against the man's sister. Even still, Alyssa considered Nathan's attitude blown out of proportion. Raising his voice might have been better than the cold treatment he displayed right then.

On Nathan's orders, Aziz went off to inform Talia of the guests sticking around, maybe even spending the night. Alyssa decided to leave the two scowling men in the foyer and to go find the women. She rounded a corner, hearing voices, and came upon Piper crying at Emma's words.

"I'm sorry. I can't take it anymore. You're ashamed of me, and I deserve better. We're through. I'm leaving."

Alyssa moaned and approached them. "I guess you haven't heard. There's a storm. We're all getting cozy tonight."

# Chapter Eleven

*A*lyssa woke from her sleep with a start. She lay on Nathan's chest and felt the slow rise and fall that said he hadn't roused. What had she heard to disturb her? A shout? The clock on the bedside table read three a.m. She climbed from the bed and tiptoed to the balcony doors to pull the curtains aside. From the look of things, the storm had passed. Down the beach, someone stumbled along. She frowned. *Don't tell me that idiot woman is out there pining over her girlfriend.*

She checked the bed behind her, and the memory of lying in Nathan's arms washed over her. The pull came on too strong, driving her to want to stay at his side or feel him on top of her again like they'd done earlier. No, she couldn't do that knowing Piper wandered outside with a broken heart. No one in her family knew the truth, so waking someone else seemed pointless. *She doesn't even like me!*

Grumbling, Alyssa pulled on the clothing she'd discarded when she and Nathan came upstairs to bed. She chose flip-flops for easy removal once she walked on the sand and then left the room. Outside, a cool wind stirred her hair. She pushed the tendrils away as she scanned the beach. Piper had disappeared. With a sigh, Alyssa turned to walk around to the front of the house, but movement to her left stopped her. Someone else was out here. She was sure she'd seen the hulking figure of a man. Fear tightened the muscles in her throat, and she forced a swallow. Time to go back in the house, where safety lay.

Clouds drifted in the sky, allowing the moon to shine brighter and illuminate the beach even more. The gentle waves lapped at the shore, giving a creepy and a peaceful feel to the night. She took a few steps back to the house, and then an unmistakable shout rang out. That had been Piper.

Alyssa ran in the direction she'd heard the woman, and this time she spotted Piper standing up from the sand. She swayed on her feet, and Alyssa shook her head. *Drunk at three in the morning and on the beach. Talk about dangerous.*

"Piper!" Alyssa picked up the pace, but the wet sand dragged at her feet and seemed deeper than previous days she'd walked there. She gained ground on the woman and opened her mouth to call out again when something jerked her from behind. She went down hard, the wind knocked out of her chest.

"Alyssa, are you okay?"

She froze. "Cullen, what are you doing out here?"

He squatted beside her, serene as if they had run into each other during the day and not the middle of the night, as if he hadn't just stopped her from helping Piper. Her heart hammered, and her mouth had gone dry. A buzzing in her head made it feel like she'd pass out any second, but by force of will, she struggled to calm down.

"I was forced to spend the night, remember?"

She peered over her shoulder in the direction she'd seen Piper. The woman had disappeared again. "I have to go. I think Piper's upset and drunk. It's not safe out here for her."

"Yeah, even a peaceful place like this can bring trouble for a woman."

She eyed him, wondering if he meant someone other than Piper—like *her*. Did he hold it against her that much because she'd turned him down? The man should be able to get any woman he wanted.

"I'm glad you understand." She stood, but he grabbed her arm. A jerk away didn't unsettle his grip, and she frowned at him. "Let me go, Cullen."

"Come riding on my boat with me."

"Are you nuts? It's the middle of the night."

"Best time. No one will disturb us."

"I don't think so. Now let me go before I scream."

For a moment, she thought he wouldn't, but he released his clasp and stepped back, holding his hands up in surrender. "See? I'm not a bad guy."

*You so* are. *I know that now.*

Rather than go on to find Piper, she started back to the house. Better to wake Nathan and tell him the truth so he could help his sister. The hair stood at her nape, and her muscles ached feeling like any second Cullen would grab her again. She made it to the back door of Nathan's house and stepped through into the cooler interior. Just as she breathed a sigh of relief, a hand slammed over her mouth from behind, followed by an arm around her waist. She screamed, but he muffled the noise and hauled her backward.

Alyssa clutched at the doorframe. If he got her outside, her chances of getting away would decrease. She kicked at his legs with no effect and tried biting the hand. He ground harder, and she tasted the metallic flavor of blood. Tears wet her cheeks. Fear closed her throat, and panic made it hard to think.

"Let go, Alyssa," he whispered in her ear. "We're going to have fun."

*You're insane. Nathan, please...*

Her fingers, burning with the effort to hold on, lost all strength. Cullen jerked her up into his arms, and she managed to wrench her mouth away. Sucking in a deep breath, she prepared to scream, but the crack across her cheek sent her head knocking into his collarbone.

"You want to try that again?" The ringing in her ears made it hard to hear him. "Now, we're going for a little ride. You'll like the boat. It's not as big as Nathan's, but I've had some extras built in that are much better than anything he has."

He tangled his hand in her hair and yanked. She whimpered. When they stepped off the patio and onto the path, hope ebbed, but the next thing she knew, she lay on the ground facedown. A scuffle ensued behind her. She rolled over and cried in relief to see Nathan. In slacks, bare chested and barefooted, her lover lifted Cullen to his toes with one hand wrapped around his neck and pounded a fist into the man's face. When Cullen went down, Nathan followed and drove blow after blow into his jaw. Cullen flailed about and then went still.

Nathan stood and hurried to her side. He took her into his arms. "Are you okay, baby?"

"I-I'm fine." She did all she could not to cry again, but failed.

He crushed her in his embrace and let her get it out.

"I don't understand why he obsessed over getting me to go on his yacht. It doesn't even make sense. Why me? Oh no, I think I'm going to be sick."

Nathan walked with her in his arms toward the house, and lights came on in several rooms. Aziz appeared in the doorway. She buried her face against Nathan's neck.

"Call the police," Nathan barked, "and bring him inside so he doesn't get away."

"Yes, sir."

"Did Felix stay because of the storm?"

"Yes, sir."

"Wake him. I'm taking Alyssa to the hospital."

She raised her head. "No, I said I'm fine. I just need to get cleaned up." The memory of his sister came back. "Piper! She was outside. Someone needs to go get her."

Nathan paled, but Talia appeared in the exit to the hall. "She's inside. Miss James found her at the front of the house."

"She's not hurt?" Nathan demanded.

"No, sir. Just…" The maid seemed embarrassed.

"Drunk." Lydia bustled in. "What's all the noise about down here? Why is everyone awake? Thank goodness I gave Leo his pain medicine. It knocks him out until morning."

"I apologize, Mom. Cullen attacked Alyssa, and I need to get her to our room so I can be sure she's okay."

Lydia's hand flew to her chest, and she sagged against Talia, who wrapped an arm about her employer. "I can't believe he would do such a thing. Are you sure? We've known him and his family for years. Why would he?"

Nathan's lips tightened, and Alyssa had the impression he knew a lot more than he chose to say about Cullen's motives. "We'll talk later. For now, I need to take care of Alyssa."

He carried her past the two women, down the hall, and up to their room.

"Put me down. I can walk."

He ignored her and sat on the bed with her on his lap. His hands explored her body, checking, she assumed, for broken bones or any other injuries. When he touched her cheek, she winced in pain and drew away.

"That asshole will die!" He started to put her aside, but she clung to him.

"No, stay with me, please." Tremors took hold of her body from every direction. She nuzzled into him, trying to stop them. "I hate this. It's not as bad as this reaction is making it seem."

"Shh, you were traumatized. The reaction is normal. I'm here, and I'm not going to leave you."

For a long while, he held her in his arms. The noise of car doors shutting outside roused Alyssa, and just when the shaking had eased, dread rose in her belly again. She'd have to recite to the police everything that happened and relive it.

Nathan rose and put her on the bed. "Sit here just a moment. I'm going to tell them to take Cullen and that you'll give a statement in the morning. Then I'll come back and help you clean up."

She nodded, but when he left, she made her way to the bathroom on her own and showered. By the time Nathan returned, she stood naked in front of the mirror surveying her face. A bruise had begun to form, and her swollen cheek squinted one eye. The split on her lip had stopped bleeding at least.

"What kind of vacation is this?" She shut her eyes to keep from giving in to another bout of tears. Nathan moved up behind her and encircled her in a warm embrace.

"I'm sorry, Alyssa. You deserve better than this."

She turned in his arms and laid her head on his shoulder.

"I told you to wait for me."

"I can take care of myself—mostly." A sob rose, but she pushed it down.

"Come on. Let me get you in bed."

With gentle care, he had her ensconced beneath the sheets and then went to shower himself. She shivered until he returned, and he pulled her into his arms.

"Nathan."

"You should sleep, Alyssa. I'll hold you until you wake."

She pushed at his chest and sat up. "I know there's something you're not telling me. I don't want to get into your business, but since it affected me, I think I have a right to know."

He sighed and ran a hand through his hair, looking away. "We have history, Cullen and I."

"What kind of history?"

Still he hesitated.

"Nathan?"

"Five years ago, there was a woman, someone who…attracted me. I did what I had to do to get her."

Alyssa stared. "What does that mean?" Her chest hurt. She wanted to take back asking him about this.

He rose from the bed and threw on a robe, then paced to the balcony doors. "Her name was Monica Devereaux. I seduced her. I told her whatever she wanted to hear just to get her to agree to have sex with me."

She cringed. "A lot of men do that. It sucks, but most women recognize the game and choose to either go along with it or tell the man to fuck off."

He sighed. "I wish it was that simple or that it ended there. The fact is…"

He swore and looked away from the beach to her. The raw expression on his face took her breath away—a mixture between regret and love. Did he still have feelings for this woman after so long? Maybe she'd told him where to stuff it and left his ass when she realized he didn't want a relationship.

"She and Cullen had been seeing each other for a couple years. Their relationship was off and on again. He loved her. I knew that."

Alyssa put a hand over her mouth. That's why Cullen was so bitter about all Nathan owned. He must have felt like he could never measure up. "I can't believe—"

"It's worse, Alyssa."

*Make it stop.*

"I shouldn't have asked." She shut her eyes and lowered her head. The discomfort in her cheek intensified. "Do you have any pain meds?"

"Damn it. I'm sorry. Let me get you something now." He disappeared from the room. While she waited for him, she thought of the possibilities. Did she get pregnant and he had a child somewhere? Obviously, she and Cullen were no longer together.

Nathan entered the room with a glass of water and pills. He handed them to her and stood over her while she swallowed them, and then took the glass to set on the nightstand. He raised her chin and examined her face. Concern darkened his eyes, and from the bulging vein in his temple, she guessed he'd like nothing more than to go to the police station and beat Cullen some more. Despite the sickening violence of it, knowing he'd protected her gave her a warm and cozy feeling.

"Better?"

She shrugged. "It'll get there." She lay in bed and pulled the sheets to her chin. Maybe if he thought she was too tired to listen, he wouldn't continue his story. Curiosity won out over fear, and she had to ask. "What's the worse thing you mentioned?"

Nathan dropped to the bed beside her and stared at nothing. "I took her out on my yacht."

A cold chill raced down Alyssa's spine.

"She—*we*—were drinking and having a good time. Then she told me she'd fallen for me. I told her I didn't feel that way about her. I thought she would take it in stride. I was wrong."

At the end, his voice went flat, unemotional, but instinct told her a lot more than indifference coursed through his mind.

"The death was ruled an accident. I was below deck at the time. I don't believe she killed herself—at least I tell myself that. One of the crewmen said he saw her leaning over the rail. He started toward her to try to convince her it wasn't safe so late at night. Several of us heard a scream. Then she was gone."

Alyssa put a hand to her mouth, but the sob escaped. Nathan reached for her, but she shook her head. "I'm okay."

"I jumped in after her when I found out. So did the crewmen. We shined lights on the water and threw in a life preserver. Over and over we dove. Nothing. Now you know the true bastard that I am and how I destroyed two lives in one night."

"Nathan."

He watched her, but she couldn't move, couldn't reach out to him and hold him to tell him it was okay. Shock kept her immobile, clutching the sheets until her fingers hurt. After some moments, he stood up and walked to the door.

"Why did Cullen single me out? I mean, I'd barely gotten here before he approached me."

He turned to face her. "For the simple fact that I've never brought a woman to meet my parents. It's possible he saw us together in New York and made some inquiries, found out I intended to bring you here, and made sure to be down here at the same time."

"Oh."

He waited in silence, and then said, "I'll arrange for you to return home tomorrow."

She didn't answer, and he left the room without another word. Going home was the right thing to do. Nathan's plan had not exactly backfired, but it hadn't gone well. Her being here meant more stress on his dad. Who knew how the old man would react upon learning she'd been attacked in his home. He needed relaxation and to be surrounded by his family. She had to go, and yet...*I've been dumb enough to fall for Nathan too—in just a few days.*

Unlike Monica Devereaux, however, she was not some weak woman who would drink herself silly or risk her life because of a broken heart. She would not confess to Nathan. After tossing back the covers, she stood to her feet and threw on a robe. The clock read four thirty. So little time had passed after so much happening. If she was going tomorrow, she wanted to spend her last hours with him. Maybe together they could forget the darkness, if just for a little while.

# Chapter Twelve

Nathan swirled the amber liquid in his glass and took a swig. No matter how hard he tried to put it from his mind, he revisited the decision to tell Alyssa about Monica. Her eyes, full of shock and revulsion, clouded his mind until he could see nothing else. He'd thought…no, it didn't matter what he thought. Cullen had hurt her because of him, and even while his blood boiled to get his hands on the man again, he deserved a beating as well. Five years ago, he had gotten off without a hitch. Correction—the law hadn't punished him for his foolishness, but the guilt weighed without mercy. Now he would have to see Alyssa home and say good-bye to her.

He downed the last of the drink and slammed it on the table before him.

"Are you going to get drunk too?"

He started, so absorbed in his thoughts he hadn't heard her enter the room. She wore a robe, and he wondered about the nightie beneath and the body beyond that. Despite plans to wipe her from his mind, he couldn't help wanting to touch and kiss her, to make love to her. Even with her bruises, she called to his lust.

"Why are you up? You should be sleeping."

"I couldn't. Not knowing you were down here alone beating yourself up."

"I'll be fine. I'm not so delicate."

She approached, padding on bare feet. He focused on those long legs and sighed.

"So you want me to leave?"

"No." *Yes, get out of here while you still can.*

She sat down in front of him, almost in his lap. The mere act had her robe rising higher, and the expanse of her creamy brown thighs watered his mouth and hardened his dick. He ran a hand over his face and reconsidered that second drink. "I'm not in the mood for talking, Alyssa."

"Who said anything about talking?"

He checked her eyes, soft and inviting. She couldn't mean to tempt him. She'd just been manhandled, threatened with...and then he knew. Her lying beneath him, his cock driven deep into her heat, that's what it would take to get through the rest of this night, until the memories receded to where he'd buried them. The same went for her. She wanted to erase the touch of a man he never should have allowed into his home. He'd known Cullen hated him because of their confrontation five years ago after Monica died, but him showing up at the house pretending to be Piper's boyfriend? That had taken him by surprise.

For a moment, he had believed it—until he saw his sister's obvious misery. When she woke from her drunken slumber, he would confront her and find out the real problem. For now, Alyssa held all of his attention, and nothing could tear him from her side.

"Come here." He held out his hand and waited. She touched fingertips to his palm, sending arrows of need coursing through his body. Soon enough he'd place her beneath him and lose himself inside her sweetness.

He leaned back on the couch, and she knelt between his legs. Her breasts strained against the thin material of her silk robe, the nipples pronounced. No way she wore a nightie, which added fire to his desire.

"Open it. Let me see."

She reared back a little and did his bidding. First the smooth shoulders came into view, provoking a memory of him kissing there and nibbling at her neck. Then those luscious breasts popped free of the material, and he swore. Damn, those nipples were big, and the areolas so dark, he craved to lick and suck until she pleaded for him to take her. His hands itched to get a touch, but he held off.

"More."

She unbelted the robe and let the filmy garment fall to the couch. A tiny waist, curvy hips, and a pussy shaved for his pleasure. *Fuck yes!*

"Spread your legs, baby. Touch it. Let me see if you're wet."

Again, she obeyed, and first ran a widespread hand over

her belly, down across her navel, and lower to her heat. She used the first and second finger to tease her clit and arched her back at the same time. The moan she uttered made him grit his teeth to stay where he was and not yank her to him. He liked her playing with herself for him.

"Inside," he commanded, and she pushed her fingers between her folds. He took it all in, watching as the digits disappeared, then slid out wet with her cream. Again, she pressed in, but he stopped her and pulled her hand away from her body. He raised it to suck on her fingers, enjoying the taste of her essence. She hissed and moaned his name. That did it. He couldn't hold back any longer. He tugged, and she fell onto his chest. Holding her head at the angle he wanted, he devoured her mouth and thrust his tongue between her lips. A swift movement had her on her back and him above her, wedged pelvis to pelvis. His cock swelled all the more when he kneed her legs apart and planted himself between them.

With fingers knotted in her hair, he kissed along her neck down to her chest. He explored lower to the beginning swell of one breast, but paused so he could enjoy the softness, the feel of the taut nipple on his cheek. Sliding a hand along her side, he leaned up to take his fill with the sight of her. So much smaller than he, Alyssa incited protectiveness, and yet, he was also the monster she needed to watch out for. He wanted to consume her, to take all she had to offer—and more.

When he could stand it no longer, he licked her nipple and felt her shiver. Sucking it between his lips, he moaned, knowing the vibrations would drive her crazy. She squirmed and clutched at his shoulders.

"Tell me you want more."

"M-More, Nathan. I want you inside me."

"Oh, you'll get my cock, my love, but not yet. Right now, I'm going to eat your pussy. Tell me how you feel about that."

She whined and raised her hips. He laid a forearm on her thigh to hold her down.

"Tell me, or you won't get it."

"I want it. Eat my pussy, Nathan."

Explosive desire knocked him off-balance. She hadn't spoken dirty to him in their previous sexual encounters. Not because he'd stopped her, but he hadn't provoked it. "Yes! I like you talking dirty, baby. Say it again. Tell me what else you want."

"Eat my pussy, and I want you to fuck me. Nathan, I want your cock inside me as deep as it goes, and I want you to fuck me hard, really hard, until I can't stand the stimulation."

His cock twitched so much he thought he'd come. He leaned down and sucked on her other nipple and let it pop from his mouth. Her thigh muscles quivered. "You're a very good girl. For that, I'm going to have to give you a special present."

He slid lower and raised her legs. She stuffed the back of her hand to her mouth, and he knew it was to head off the coming scream. One lave at her nether lips had her keening. He took his time, first gathering the cream streaming from her sex and then working his tongue higher until he met her clit. She arched her back and cried out his name when he took the tiny bud into his mouth and gave it a little suck. When he let go, she protested, but he had to get his fill looking at her. Such dark chocolate, wet from his mouth and her juices. He stroked it from top to bottom and then sucked his own fingers so he could delve inside without hurting her. She whimpered and squirmed, but he pushed deeper. Her warmth surrounded him, and he remembered the feel cocooning his cock, milking it for his own juices.

He let his head fall forward on her thigh, and he shut his eyes. A deep breath took in the scent of her essence. Alyssa didn't know it, but she had full control of him. He'd give her whatever she wanted. How had he come to this place, wanting—no *needing*—a woman the way he did her. Thoughts of her consumed him, and to imagine letting her go once they were back in New York brought devastation and rage.

*Calm down, Nathan. To have a woman such as her, no, that didn't bear fantasizing on. Just enjoy it for the time it lasts.*

He patted her pussy, giving it a light smack. She moaned and raised her hips. He pushed them back down and spanked her sweetness again. The slight sting seemed to take her to the edge. She would not last much longer. He leaned in and drew in her intoxicating aroma once more and then delved his tongue between her folds. With greedy hunger, he slid his tongue up her channel and pushed his nose against her clit. While he ate, he teased her bud, turning his head back and forth in tiny movements. She began fighting him, trying to raise her hips, tugging at his hair. A cry of pleasure left her throat, and then the quivering started and didn't stop. Her thighs trapped his head between them. He didn't let up but reached beneath her to cup her ass cheeks. Driving her tighter to his mouth, he ate and ate. Then it came—her raging orgasm, tearing through her, forcing control from her grip. He raised one of her thighs and kept laving that clit until she begged for mercy. Only then did he sit up and stare into her flushed face with satisfaction.

"Now I take what you owe me," he informed her.

An eyebrow arched, and she put a foot in the middle of his chest. His cock strained for entry to her. The feigned resistance from her skyrocketed his desire.

"You're going to fight me?"

She smirked. "I don't think I have the energy."

He smacked her ass, making her yelp. "Good, because all I require you to do is spread your legs."

Her eyes flashed. "Bastard."

He grinned. "You love it."

"You're telling me what I feel?"

"Now you're being a bad girl, sassing me. I think I need to punish you."

They stared at one another for a bit, and he waited for her reaction, hoping she'd try something. When she sat up as if to escape and grabbed for her robe, he snatched the garment from her and threw it to the floor. She twisted away from him, but this time he encouraged her in it by forcing her over until she lay flat on the couch facedown. He smacked her ass, and the hot and sexy part of her body rose, probably without her meaning for it to. Another *thwack* echoed in the room when he brought his hand down on the soft flesh. She scratched at the upholstery, trembling.

He stroked that sweet little ass and then bent down to give each cheek a kiss. When he began kissing his way up her back, she moaned. He lay above her, spooning her ass. Rather than remove his robe and boxers, he shoved the material aside and knocked her legs wider with his knees. After all they'd done and how much they teased each other, he could not hold back. He stared down at her ass while he guided his cock into her pussy. So wet and inviting, it sucked him in until he lay buried to the hilt.

"Fuck," he growled and pushed harder. He covered her hands with his and curled her fingers into her palms. Leaning up, he pulled back almost to the tip of his cock and then jammed forward again. The impact of their bodies coming together sent bolts of pleasure throughout his groin. He withdrew and thrust once more, then again until he pounded nonstop into her pussy. He forgot everything— everything except the feel of claiming her body, making her his own, and not letting up until he found his release.

"You want me to stop?" he demanded in her ear.

"Never!"

He crossed her arms over her chest, still holding her hands, and brought his weight down on her. The springs in the couch creaked in protest as he thrust inside her heat. Beneath him, Alyssa gasped and turned her head toward the door. He ignored the sound he'd heard as well. Daylight pierced the windows, and someone stirred in the house.

"Nathan, someone's awake."

He released her hand and ran fingers along her abdomen. Still, he drove his dick home. He would not stop even if his parents walked into the room. His orgasm began to build, and he gasped for breath. Something dropped in the hall. He raised one thigh to push Alyssa's higher. Staring down at the their bodies, he took in the sight of how they molded together, her ass wedged into his pelvis as if they'd never separate again. Arching and pumping in unison, they fucked, and he loved every second, even the threat of being caught.

"Nathan," she moaned, and that did it. He thrust one last time and held it. His come exploded from his cock and flooded her channel. He pushed harder, deeper, then reached down her front to pinch her clit. She shouted through a second orgasm.

"That's better." He rose and pulled her to her feet. She glared at him, but he only chuckled. "Didn't you enjoy that?"

She bent to grab her robe from the floor, and he enjoyed the curvy ass and the spreading of her pussy lips, now spilling with both their essences. To his disappointment, the view disappeared when she pulled her robe on and belted it with such vehemence, he couldn't help laughing again.

"Someone was probably out there listening, you know."

He shrugged. "I hope they enjoyed themselves. Now, come on. I want you to get some rest before eleven."

"Eleven?"

He led her to the door and opened it. "Yes, the police station."

"Okay, I guess we have to do it."

157

"Don't worry. I'll be there by your side the entire time. You can lean on me."

The softness in her eyes almost made him believe she loved him, but no, he'd told her the truth about what he did. Even if she had warm feelings before that, he'd killed them. Neither of them could deny the sexual desire, but it was all they had, and soon it would come to an end.

⌒

Nathan leaned back in his seat with Alyssa at his side. His parents chatted across from him, and Piper occupied a chair near the window, away from the rest of them. He had an urge to pull Alyssa onto his lap, but resisted.

"So how did everything go at the police station?" his dad asked, interrupting his thoughts.

He considered how much to share in an effort to keep his dad from getting upset. "Fine. He was charged with felony assault and attempted kidnapping. I'm also going to talk to a doctor friend of mine and see if he can't do up an affidavit stating he recommends Cullen get a psych eval and take it Tony Davis."

His father nodded in agreement. "The judge?"

"Yes. He owes me a favor anyway."

Alyssa blinked up at him. "You know a judge?"

"I do."

She stared at him a little while longer, and he knew she did some judging of her own for the lifestyle he led. Never in his life had he questioned how he lived or even the money he had until he met Alyssa. If he were an average Joe, would she stay with him? *Wait, what am I thinking here?*

"Well, some have called me flighty," his mother said, "but I'm not stupid. You don't seem to be broken up over Cullen's betrayal, Piper."

His sister turned from the window. "I don't hate her enough to want her hurt, if that's what you're getting at."

Nathan clenched his jaw and uttered in a low warning, "No one assumed you hated Alyssa at all."

Piper's gaze shifted from their parents to him, and he saw the fear. Her fingers gripped the arms of her chair, and then she straightened her back. "He wasn't my boyfriend."

No one spoke. He hoped she wouldn't leave the pronouncement there.

"Emma was my girlfriend."

His mother waved her hand, and Nathan figured she thought Piper meant in the sense of being a friend who was female. The two women had been that way for years, and no one needed it pointed out.

Piper licked her lips and glanced at Alyssa. Now he went on alert.

"Emma was my *girlfriend*...I mean, she was my lover. Not Cullen."

His dad started in surprise, his mother's hand flew to her mouth, but there was no reaction from the woman at his side. He raised the hand he held on Alyssa's shoulder and tangled fingers in her hair. She shivered, and he let a few strands flow between his digits. So his sister was gay. A number of past incidents sped through his mind, clues to her preference, and while he wasn't sure what he felt about her announcement, Alyssa remained at the forefront of his concerns.

"Piper, I don't understand this," his mother complained, sounding tearful.

His dad hadn't said a word, and from the set of his mouth, he wouldn't anytime soon. The feminine voices rose. Nathan blew out a sigh and leaned forward.

"Enough!"

Both women fell silent midsentence. His mother glared at him in reproach, but he ignored it. Piper's gaze accused him of siding with his mother, which was ridiculous given he hadn't voiced an opinion. "Mom, don't you think you should discuss this later?"

Alyssa popped to attention. "Oh, I can get out of your way."

He dragged her back to his side. "Not you," he growled.

His mother cast a fleeting glance at his father. "You're right. Piper, you just took us by surprise. Let's talk about it later and have a nice, enjoyable time on Alyssa's last day."

Piper stood. "I'm sorry, but I have to go. Because I was too scared to tell you the truth, Emma broke up with me. I'm going to go talk to her to get her back."

"Piper, don't you dare," his mother screeched.

His sister apologized again, surprising him. For the first time, even while she defied their parents, she appeared more mature than he'd ever seen her. She wasn't throwing a fit or being rebellious. She respectfully disagreed with their parents while holding to her decision. He admired her for that, and something told him the desirable little imp beside him had a hand in it. Maybe he should keep her.

After Piper vacated the room, he stood as well and pulled Alyssa to her feet. "If you'll excuse us, Mom and

Dad, I need to talk to Alyssa alone. Okay if we meet back here around dinnertime?"

His dad laid a hand over his mother's. "Go ahead, son. Mom and I will be fine."

Nathan heard the anger in his tone and considered staying, but left them to it. He led Alyssa out to the back of the house, and the two of them removed their shoes.

"You're going to ruin your pants," she chided.

"I'm rolling them up."

She chuckled, but it seemed a bit hollow. "I thought you had a business meeting dressed like that."

"I did. I canceled."

She straightened, and she'd never looked more beautiful in the simple white sundress. He took her hand and led her out to the beach. A breeze stirred her hair, and he pushed it back only to have it cover one eye again. Already the swelling on her cheek had begun to recede, but the bruising remained. He needed to work harder to protect her. Maybe as an official boyfriend, he would have that right on an ongoing basis.

"You knew, didn't you?"

Her eyes widened. "Knew what?"

"Don't play coy, Alyssa. Piper's admission didn't surprise you. Why?"

She sighed. "I caught them talking in the restaurant when we went shopping. She and Emma were arguing, and Emma begged her to tell you and your parents. Piper thought I was going to tell you, but it wasn't my secret to reveal. I did end up advising her to start acting like a woman and not a spoiled child."

He nodded. So he'd been correct guessing Alyssa's influence. "I want us to make it real between us," he blurted.

His sudden change of subject appeared to catch her off guard. She stared at him. "What?"

He reached out and tugged her to him. No matter how hard he tried, he couldn't keep his hands off her. "I said, I want us to make this real. I want you to be mine—on a long-term basis."

"Yours?"

She stepped out of his hold and turned to walk down the beach. He followed, frustration eating at him. When he reached her, he fell into step beside her rather than force her into his arms. The crease between her eyebrows said she struggled with his suggestion. Perhaps she couldn't look beyond his past after all, and he couldn't blame her.

"Alyssa—"

"We already had this discussion, Nathan. I told you. I'm not going to be your mistress. The mere thought of it denotes you taking care of me financially and me giving it up in exchange."

"Who said anything about you being my mistress?"

She stopped walking. "Well what were you talking about?"

He hitched his shoulders and stuffed his hands in his pockets. She'd been right. The pants he'd rolled up had uncurled, and now the ends were crusted with wet sand. *Forget the pants. This is your chance.* Being nervous with a woman was foreign. He'd always commanded control and set the pace of the relationship, if one existed. No, that was just it. He'd never had a relationship per se, but keeping Alyssa in his life dictated it.

"I want you as my girlfriend as well as my lover."

Her mouth fell open, and her eyes widened. She stuttered unintelligible words for a few moments, and he began to hope she would say yes. After all, she understood what he wanted, which he dared to guess was what she desired as well.

"No."

His world fell apart. "Come again?"

She took a step back from him as if she suspected he would attack. A rush of—was it pain?—constricted his chest. He would never hurt her, and it killed him to think she'd fear him. "Alyssa."

She held up her hands to ward him off when he raised his to touch her. He stopped midmotion. The full lips thinned, and the jaw set. Her narrowed gaze never left his face. "I did it for the money."

He blinked. "What money?"

"I did it for the money," she repeated. "I came here and pretended to be your girlfriend for twenty thousand dollars to save my bookstore."

What she said might as well be gibberish. "I didn't offer to pay you."

"I know that, damn it!" Her hands slid to her hips. "When Trinity couldn't come, or rather her boyfriend had a problem with it, I offered to instead in exchange for a loan from her to help me make some updates to my store. I didn't tell you, and I asked her not to tell you because it's my business, and—"

"You thought I would look down on you. Do you think so little of me?"

163

"Of course not."

"You didn't sleep with me because—"

The intensity of her scowl cut off his words. "I'm not selling my body for anybody! The sex was good, and I did it because we were attracted to each other. I don't deny that, but that's just where it has to end. I'm sorry, Nathan. I like you, but there can't be any more between us. Please, I want to go home."

So there it was. The first time he'd offered a woman more, and she turned him down. He couldn't say he didn't see it coming. In her own way, Alyssa was prejudiced, and there wasn't a damn thing he could do to change it. He would miss her. Even as she walked ahead of him to the house, he saw his hope ebb and die, and defeat weighed heavy on his shoulders.

# Chapter Thirteen

So you turned him down?"

"Trin, don't look at me like that," Alyssa complained and shifted the food on her plate from one side to the other. They sat having lunch, but Alyssa hadn't taken more than a couple bites of the juicy steak. She really should since her cousin footed the bill. "I did the right thing for me."

"The right thing?" Her cousin shook her head, disbelief plain in her expression. "You click with the sexiest man alive—Curtis aside. He's rich, generous, and wants to be with you, and the right thing to do is turn him down? I don't get that. Please explain it to me."

Alyssa grunted. "You wouldn't understand."

"Try me."

Alyssa spread her hands, trying to think of the right words. "We come from two different worlds…"

"And you're intimidated by his."

"What!"

"You feel like you don't fit in and never will."

"I don't get why you're saying that, Trinity. I thought you were on my side."

Her cousin said nothing to this.

"Okay, let me explain. We went to this party, and he said it was a beach party. I assumed it would be on the beach. It was in a ritzy hotel, and everybody was dressed up. Then I went to a real beach party, and it was fun. I even walked on the beach at night with this guy that turned out to be crazy, but aside from that—"

Trinity burst out laughing. "Aside from the crazy?"

"I'm saying I had my views, and he had his. A couple times we didn't see eye to eye on how I should respond to certain things."

"Girl, please. Curtis and I don't see eye to eye on a lot, and he is so not rich. Neither am I. That's people. Admit that you're scared to be hurt again, and because Nathan is who he is, you feel like it's more likely you'll get hurt."

She slumped in her chair and let her fork clatter to her plate. "I hate admitting all of that is true, but it is. Something bad happened to him in the past, and I feel like he can't be serious because of it."

"Did he say that?"

"No."

"Then don't assume. You like him?"

Alyssa bit her lip and dipped her head. She shut her eyes and recalled the words Nathan spoke when he asked her to be his girlfriend. He never said he liked her let alone loved her. Not that she expected love this early in the game. *This early?* Should she expect any more, or better yet, *try* for any more? Maybe like Trinity had inferred, she'd chickened out before even giving the man a chance. From the start she judged him and found him lacking. Not in the looks or the ability arena, but in the boyfriend material sense. She was afraid, and no one could fault her for that. Everyone at some point had been hurt, and many were scared to try again. The biggest issue she had was that she...*I love him. Already. This soon. I must be crazy.* And yet, she could tell. With Trinity's words, she knew she would give him a chance. That is, if he still wanted her after she'd shut him down in the islands.

"You think he's a real good guy?"

Trinity rolled her eyes. "I've known Nathan for three years. He likes women, and he's never without a partner."

Alyssa cringed.

"But!" She reached across the table and took Alyssa's hand in hers. "I've never seen the man so busted after having a fling with one, and he's been grouchy as hell at the office lately. I'm thinking it has something to do with you. So my question is, what are you going to do about it?"

"I'm not sure." She stood up and gathered her things. "Thanks for lunch, Trin, but there's something I have to do."

Trinity cast her a knowing look, which Alyssa ignored and hurried out of the restaurant. She tugged her phone from her pocket and headed down the street. Her cousin had informed her she'd taken the rest of the day off to spend time with Curtis on his, who usually worked on the weekends. With Trinity out, maybe she could run in to see Nathan. Not until she reached the executive suite of his company did she realize he might not be available, since even in the Caribbean he'd dealt with constant meetings.

"I'm here. I might as well go in, I guess." She shifted her shoulders to relieve stress and pushed the glass doors open. When she reached Trinity's office, she found another woman she hadn't seen before sitting behind the desk. A moment of panic made her recheck the nameplate, and she breathed a sigh of relief. Trinity's name still curled in etched gold letters on the plate.

"Good afternoon, may I help you?" the woman said.

Alyssa hesitated, still dealing with nerves. "Um, yes, is Nathan in?"

"*Mr.* Corde is in with someone right now. Do you have an appointment?"

Was it Alyssa's imagination that she'd heard the emphasis on "mister" as if this heifer corrected her? "No, I don't normally need one." Now she was getting bold, which was laughable.

Offense radiated off the woman, and Alyssa couldn't figure out her attitude problem. She glanced down at herself and then realized she'd shown up in a T-shirt and shorts. Damn, she probably looked a mess, but she'd been cleaning out some stock at the store and preparing space for new books and equipment. Trinity's invite to lunch had come without notice, but she'd thought since it was her cousin, she didn't need to dress up, not when she would go back to work and continue what she'd begun that morning. No way would she go in to see Nathan like this.

She started to turn away. "I'm going to give him a call later."

Embarrassment made her steps awkward, and when a door opened somewhere behind her and to the right, she froze. A tinkling laugh that seemed familiar made her glance over her shoulder. Nathan filled the doorway to his office, and the skank Natasha laid a hand on his chest, too intimate for Alyssa not to stagger with a stab of pain to her midsection.

"You're silly, Nathan," Natasha teased.

"I wasn't trying to be," was Nathan's sharp reply, and Alyssa looked into his face. Her eyes widened to catch a less than impressed expression at Natasha's playfulness. In fact, he appeared more annoyed than anything. Still, she hurried to take her leave before he spotted her. She made it less than a couple yards from the glass doors.

"Alyssa."

She halted at his voice, the deep timbre going through her and doing things to her body that brought to mind all the times they'd made love. Why had she come here? To face him took an eternity, one she wished would go on forever. Better yet, if she'd never stepped through the door, this insecurity wouldn't choke her now.

"What are you doing here?"

For some reason she thought he'd show the emotion Trinity had claimed he'd been feeling missing her, but his expression remained closed. Nothing more than mild curiosity showed, making her wonder if her cousin had lied just to let Alyssa make a fool of herself.

When she could find no words, he continued. "Trinity took the rest of the day off."

"Um, I know," she muttered. "We had lunch."

His brows rose, and he appeared about to say more when Natasha sidled up to him and clung to his arm, pressing her breast against it. A nasty sense of déjà vu came over Alyssa, and she gritted her teeth.

"Oh, it's you," Natasha simpered, "the little bookstore owner." The way she said it made it sound like Natasha discovered a roach had crawled in from the street.

If Nathan had shown no emotion a moment before, the floodgates opened in that second. He wrenched his arm from Natasha's hold, almost knocking her to the floor. "Apologize! Now!"

Both Alyssa and Natasha gasped. Natasha pouted up at him and took a step in his direction. The piercing light in his eyes could have singed the hair off the woman's head if it had the power. Natasha wobbled on her spiky heels and halted.

"I won't repeat myself," Nathan ground out.

Natasha spun to face Alyssa with moist eyes. "I'm sorry. I didn't mean to insult you."

*Like hell you didn't.* Alyssa didn't say a word, and Nathan seemed to notice that as well, as if because she didn't forgive the woman for her insincere apology, neither would he.

"Get out, Natasha," he added. "And if you don't leave without another word, I will call security to have you escorted from the building."

Seeing the seriousness in his gaze, the woman almost ran for the door. When she disappeared through it, Alyssa cast a hesitant glance at Nathan. "I heard you were grumpy, but…"

"Not toward you."

The simple sentence hung between them. She became

aware the woman replacing Trinity for the day stared at them in her office doorway. Nathan took her hand and led her to his door. She passed through and heard the door click shut behind her. The nerves started up again, and she twisted her fingers together.

He strode up and rested his hands on her shoulders. She dared not turn and look into his face.

"Tell me why you're here."

The words flowed over her like a caress. A fantasy of him kissing her neck and nibbling at her ear flowed through her mind. She tried coming back to reality and just managed it with supreme effort.

"I wanted to tell you…" She licked her lips.

"Yes?"

"I-If your offer is still on the table…" No way she felt brave enough to admit she loved him. "I want to be your girlfriend."

He spun her to face him and tipped her chin higher. She gulped. When he stared into her eyes, it was as if he bared her soul whether she wanted it uncovered or not.

"Do you love me, Alyssa?"

*Unfair!*

"Love?"

"Yes, love." He stepped closer, and the heat from his body warmed her, exciting desire. "I see something in your eyes, and I dare to believe it's love."

She tugged from his touch and moved closer to his desk. Leaning on the heavy wood gave her much-needed support. "Don't you think it's a little early to talk about love? I mean, we haven't been seeing each other that long."

He remained where he stood and folded powerful arms over an even more impressive chest. She wanted to pant with longing, but held on to her dignity.

"Love doesn't take weeks of getting to know a person, or even months. It's a decision."

She curled one side of her lip. "A decision?"

He grinned, and the sun shone in that room. "Yes, a decision. You make the choice to open your heart, and in an instant—love. That choice might not come until you feel at ease with the other person, but the end result is instantaneous."

"Funny, I never pegged you for the love-at-first-sight type."

Now he strode toward her, taking his time, tempting and teasing with just his presence. He held out a hand, and before she realized what she did, her palm lay in his. He drew her to him and wrapped an arm around her waist. His cock hardened, and her pussy responded, moistened and ready.

"I loved you the first time I saw you, Alyssa."

Her mouth fell open. He kissed the tip of her nose.

"What? That's not possible. I...We...You met me when I came to the office the first time. That was months ago."

"Indeed."

"That's not possible," she repeated stupidly.

"And yet, I love you."

She hung on to his jacket with clenched fingers. "Nathan."

"I love you, Alyssa."

"Stop saying that. Wait, no, don't stop." Her head spun.

"Did you get Trinity to pretend she would go with you to the Cayman Islands only to manipulate me into going?"

"No, of course not. Although it couldn't have worked out better. I had no false pretenses, but I wondered how I would kiss her when I needed you." He nuzzled her neck just as she'd wanted to feel moments ago. She dipped her head back and shut her eyes. The craving for so much more overwhelmed her.

"Nathan."

"Say it again, my love."

She shivered. "This is too much to believe. Someone like you…"

"I'm only a man. Nothing more, nothing less." He raised his head to look into her eyes. "Can you say it?"

"Your name?"

He shook his head. "I'll get you to say that soon enough when I make love to you."

Her knees jellied, and she clung tighter.

"Say you love me."

What did she have to lose? This man, an amazing man, who was everything she wanted, loved her. He had admitted it.

"Why did you ask me to be your mistress?"

"I never said I didn't make mistakes, baby."

She rested her forehead on his chest. "I love you, Nathan."

"Again," he pleaded, and she heard the emotion choking him.

She looked him in the eye. "I love you so much, and you're right. It can happen in an instant. I *love* you."

173

Her feet left the floor when he swooped her off them and into his arms. He swung her around the room trapped in a bear hug, but she didn't want to escape. They kissed, lips meeting and then their tongues. She tasted him, moaning and wrapping her arms around his neck. When he stopped spinning, he didn't let her down, but pulled her legs up to encircle his hips. He walked forward until her ass touched the desk, and he sat her on it, never relinquishing her lips.

"Mm," he moaned, "you taste so good. I want to kiss you until I'm drunk."

"Don't stop on my account." She grinned up at him and tugged his tie until his lips met hers. He gave in to her demand.

"Take off your shorts."

"Are you nuts? Not here."

He leaned back and ran a hand between them to cup her pussy. She whimpered in bliss.

"Are you sure?"

"Nathan, that's not fair."

She stopped him from unbuttoning her shorts. "No way, buddy. I know you own the place, but still." She hopped from the desk. "Tonight. My place. I'll cook for you. Then again, on second thought, it's not safe in my area for you."

He frowned. "I'm not some delicate pretty boy."

She laughed. "Well, you're a pretty boy. I meant for your car. I've seen it. That thing would be on blocks before the night's out."

Concern darkened his eyes. "Then you'll move in with me."

"Whoa, whoa." She held up her hands and took a step back. "You're moving too fast."

He advanced toward her, and for some reason, she felt like prey. "If it's unsafe for me, it's definitely unsafe for you, Alyssa."

"I'm used to it."

He grunted. "We'll talk about it. For now, how about you spend the night at my house and cook me dinner there?"

She grinned. "Deal."

"Alyssa?"

With her hand on the door to leave, she stopped when he called her name. "Yes?"

"I know you're still nervous about my position, but I intend to win you over by any means necessary."

A thrill of anticipation raced down her back. She knew he meant if it took his money to make her accept his status, he would use it. Now that she'd admitted to herself and him she loved him, nothing would keep her from looking past her hang-ups to be with him. Sure, independence defined her, but she was more than her net worth, and so, she realized, was he. She looked forward to learning all she could about Nathan Corde.

"That reminds me. How did things go with Piper?"

He frowned and ran a hand through his hair. "A work in progress. Piper is back with Emma, and the two have decided to move in together. Because of this, my dad has cut her off."

Alyssa's hand flew to her mouth. "No!"

"Yes, and my mom is in agreement with him. I think she will come around, but we have to work on Dad."

She returned to his side and hugged him. "There's not much time…"

"I know." His jaw tensed. "I will make him see she's too important to lose at a time like this. Meanwhile, I'll make sure she never wants for anything."

Her heart warmed to him. "What's the chance of you taking the rest of the day off?"

A slow smile spread over his face. "The odds are excellent."

# Prologue

*Eight months later…*

Alyssa stretched her arms above her head and yawned. She climbed out of bed and walked over to the dresser where Nathan had set aside drawers for her. Although she slept at his house more often than not, she hadn't officially moved in, and she wouldn't, not for a while yet. She tugged the drawer open and scrounged around for her pills. When she found them, she popped one from the case and put it on her tongue.

"What's that?"

She jumped at Nathan's voice just behind her.

"Don't scare me like that. It's birth control."

He frowned. "I didn't think you were on those. I assumed you meant you were not ovulating at the time."

"Oh, really. That's the conclusion you came to?" She acknowledged his familiarity with the female body and eyeballed him, liking the scruff about his usually clean-shaved jaw, but that wasn't important about now. "So why have you been happily making love to me without a condom—and for a while now?"

He raised his eyebrows and shrugged. The innocent act didn't fool her.

"You're trying to get me pregnant, you sneak."

"Me?"

"Yes, you." She couldn't hold back the laugh. "Don't you think we should talk about it before you try to knock me up?"

"Marry me."

"Nathan! Aren't you at least a little afraid?"

"Of what?"

"Of…changing your mind?"

"No."

"What about me changing mine?"

He led her back to the bed, which wasn't a surprise. Rising each morning took one or two false starts because Nathan liked to haul her back into it for early morning sex. She complained only to cover her own desire.

He laid her down on the bed and hovered above her. Just having him stare at her naked form brought her nipples to rigid peaks and had her pussy weeping. "I won't let that happen, even if I have to seduce you. You're mine, Alyssa, and I have no intention of giving you up."

A shiver sped down her spine when he spread her legs and thumbed her clit. "Say yes."

"Nathan."

He bent down and flicked the tip of his tongue over her bud. A delve between the folds of her heat brought her hips up off the bed. He laved her juices, making her moan and cry out his name.

"T-That's playing dirty."

He squeezed the back of one thigh and licked some more. She scratched at the sheets.

"Say yes, my love."

She sat up and shoved at his shoulders before sliding away. "I want to think about it with a level head." When she turned to climb off the bed, his hand shot out, and he dragged her to her back and dropped down on top of her. No matter how she struggled, she couldn't free herself. The protest that rose to her lips died as his tongue pushed into her mouth. At the same time, he parted her thighs and thrust his cock deep and hard into her pussy.

"Yes, yes, Nathan. Wait, no."

He pulled out, and she almost screamed in protest, but he only flipped her over and drove in again. Pounding against her ass, he didn't let up. He pinned her hands to the mattress and took her body without mercy. She arched to push her ass in the air. He never played fair, and she always gave in to his demands because they felt so good.

When he got up from the bed and dragged her to the edge, she didn't resist. He stood behind her and parted her swollen nether lips with one hand and guided his shaft into her with the other. One knee on the bed, he drove in repeatedly.

A powerful orgasm took hold from her core and spread down her thighs and up across her belly. She whimpered and writhed, panting for breath. Nathan splayed a hand over her ass and crammed her sex with his dick. He held still, and soon the familiar warmth filled her. She reached beneath her hip to pinch her clit for a second, smaller orgasm and then collapsed against the bed. Nathan rolled away.

"I—"

He covered her lips with one finger. "Shh. When you say yes, it will be what you want and not because I satisfied you sexually."

Her heart burst with joy, and she hid her face in the sheets.

*Yes, Nathan. Definitely yes! To being your wife and having your children.* If ever she had wondered, she knew now. Rich or poor, Nathan was her one and only. Now and forever.

*The End*

# About the Author

**Tressie Lockwood** has always loved books, and she enjoys writing about heroines who are overcoming the trials of life. She writes straight from her heart, reaching out to those who find it hard to be completely themselves no matter what anyone else thinks. She hopes her readers enjoy her short stories.

Visit Tressie on the web at www.tressielockwood.com.